THREE WINTER GHOSTS

Gary Sargent was born in Benfleet, Essex and educated at the universities of Wales and Oxford. He lives with his wife and daughter just outside the city of Oxford, UK. Though he has lived there for over twenty years, he does not think that he has met a ghost in the aging city, but sometimes it's difficult to tell.

He is also the author of *The Ofsted Murders*, and can be contacted at grsar77@yahoo.co.uk.

THREE WINTER GHOSTS

By

Gary Sargent

TenPenny Publications
Oxford

THREE WINTER GHOSTS

....

First Published in the UK by TenPenny, 2013
This edition published 2013

ISBN: 1492931330
ISBN-13: 978-1492931331

www.threewinterghosts.com

For Emma.

Ddb...

One

I killed Jardine early on one October evening as a cold wind blew through the streets of Oxford and swept away the last bits of the summer. Clouds of yellow dust brought from God knows where by tourist feet, playbills from college garden *Tempests* and *Lears*, flyers from clubs on the Cowley road, and any vestige of heat held in the stone of the old buildings all flew before it, and tired Oxford settled and turned itself towards the coming winter.

I did it in the Senior Common Room with drink and good humour and uncharacteristic malice, smiling all the while over the rim of my wine glass as he talked and talked, digging himself in deeper. I shepherded and manoeuvred him with the easy grace of the drunk; with a deftness that makes me ashamed. At intervals I suffered an hallucinatory vision, from his point of view, of my teeth, magnified by the goblet I held, elongated and ready to bite him. He said-

"But it's also smart-phones, and instant communication, instant *information* on any subject. These things have killed the ghost story, made it irrelevant. All is explicable, and quickly."

His insufferable round face, grinned out from the winged chair. His belongingness in this brandy-bowl of a room, amongst the dun colours and elderly leather, fuelled my viciousness. He looked as if the mother ship had called him home. I prodded him again, making sure he said all the wrong things-

"But ghost stories survived gaslight, and electric lights. The Victorians were scientists and engineers – but they loved them. Why would they die out now?"

He grinned as rain began to tick from the windows and drip in the gutters, and knowledge baked out of him, as if he were an oven with the door opened wide. This was his chance – most of the College's great and good were here, idly listening to him hold forth, soaking up his apparent erudition, his easy deftness. I was gifting to him, my rival for a Junior Fellowship, the chance to be memorable to all those who mattered, and he took my gift as if it were the most natural thing in the world, as if it were his due, a tribute I owed him because of his intellect. He underestimated me.

"There's no room for magical thinking in a world that also contains the spam mail," he said. "The world has become utterly prosaic. The fears that powered the ghost story – darkness, being alone, being faced with the inexplicable, have all died away. That's why we've seen the rise of slasher flicks, and torture porn rolled out every Halloween; those films work because everyone is still afraid of pain. But you can't be menaced by a face at the window, or a hand under your bed if you can reach out to your phone and with a few keystrokes instantly connect to the entire world. Worse, if you can film the face at the window and instantly share it with thousands of reassuringly sceptical onlookers."

He swilled his wine around in his glass in an apparently expert fashion then drank it down, glancing around to gauge the room's appreciation of his argument; to me it seemed impregnable.

"Spectres melt away in the glow from the screen of your laptop. Culture has evolved beyond the reach of the common ghost."

Prick.

There was a spider that lived its entire life behind the grate of my grandmother's coal fire. Always in the dark, it had lost all pigmentation from its body. It terrified me as a child; a white skeleton spider, pale and deadly, ready to come out of the dark; a hateful winter-thing that would kill me if it could, if only it could find me on my own.

Noble came forwards in his chair, seeming to form out of a well of darkness, and I saw the spider skittering amongst the coal.

"And the uncommon ghost?" he asked, in his wheezing paper-thin voice.

Jardine turned to him, a presence in the far corner, still half-smiling, some witticism at the ready; but Noble was the most senior academic in the room and so he thought better of it. He shot a measuring glance at me, perhaps understanding at last that I had lured him into making a fool of himself. In the company of many others in the room, Jardine had made the mistake of forgetting that Noble, valiant Noble, poor cancer-ridden Noble, author of *The Ghost at the Feast*, was with us still. Poor Noble's last book, his *final* book had been badly received, roundly condemned as an irrelevance in exactly the terms that Jardine had just outlined.

Sudden embarrassment around us. The terror of Noble's nearly-dead countenance, the sharp line of his jaw, his unnatural pallor. People turned away, or to each other to murmur their dissatisfaction at Jardine's appalling insensitivity.

"I didn't mean... " he began, but Noble cut him off, tapping the end of his stick on the floorboards. It was a blow with little force behind it, yet it quelled all movement in the room.

"Malice," he said.

Noble's eyes glittered with a vapid life as he took the two of us in. A master of the dramatic gesture, a skill honed during a lifetime spent in dusty lecture halls, he chuckled and hunched forwards in his chair, leaning on his stick, all angles; a collection of broomsticks housed in a tweed suit. He said it again, slowly, as if tasting the word-

"Malice." His teeth were yellow and his tongue was grey.

"It comes from the past, or from pain... Or from people." He gulped a breath. "Ghosts are powered by malice, by the fear that they... They want..."

He coughed twice, with horrible concentration, holding himself and trying to keep the motion of his body to a minimum.

"Steady on Morris," One of the murmurers spoke up, well meaning and comforting, moving towards him with a kindly hand outstretched.

When he had calmed, and with the murmurer's hand on the small of his back, Noble looked up again; his glance passed over me, then fixed on Jardine.

"You aren't frightened by the idea that someone, or that some *thing* wishes you harm then, Dr. Jardine? Eh?"

A streetlight shone in through the Rector's window, through the coloured glass there, and put odd shapes on him in white, green and red. "That something filled with the most terrible and inhuman malice, that something implacable means to have you suffer, to exact a vengeance more awful than any crime could warrant." He moistened his lips. "As a modern man, with a mobile phone and wireless broadband, the idea does not give you pause?"

After what he had said, Jardine could hardly back down.

"No. It definitely does not."

"Good."

Noble had lost a lot of weight very quickly and his smile was fixed and ghastly. He might have been aiming for ironic, or whimsical. To me it seemed a hungry skeletal grin that could have split his head in two.

"I used to be a rational man," he said. "No gods. Few monsters. In my early career I interviewed hundreds, thousands probably, of people who believed with all their hearts that they had experienced something that was outside the scope of rational enquiry. I told myself that I was detached, only documenting, theorising. I did not judge them. But I did."

"Life can blast away one's rationality. Things can happen that overwhelm detachment. Really, no matter what I wrote, no matter how cleverly I couched my analysis, I thought them all stupid and credulous; mediaeval peasants to a man. Then something happened to make me see that their view of life was the right one."

Jardine offered only a faint smile and a, perhaps involuntary, shake of the head.

"Am I a mediaeval peasant, Dr. Jardine?"

"Of course not, and I did not mean to suggest such a thing. I'm sure that belief and stories are different."

"Are they, then?" Noble leaned forwards in his chair, still eager to lecture now that his college workload had fallen to Williams and Bohne-Khan.

"Could I tell you a story, perhaps?"

Murmurs of assent all around, and I found myself nodding. Humouring a dying man? No, not wholly humouring, because that implies that we were patronising him. Anthropology, even social anthropology, sat outside of the traditional arts and sciences divide, and touched many other disciplines.

About half of the college had sat in one of Noble's lectures at one time or another, and his stories were always worth listening to. Plus there was a rightness, a *fit* to the proposal, as the rain ran down the college windows and the wind blew its familiar mournful note over the gutters of the library. It was right; an early threnody; something for the college to remember him by.

Noble shifted in his seat, letting the light put deep shadows on the lean planes of his face, hiding his eyes. He was a craftsman, and I appreciated the spectacle of it. I saw two or three people take the opportunity to refresh their glasses, and Dobrey, the Bursar leaned forwards and murmured something into Noble's ear. Noble nodded reassuringly. He was okay. He could do this, *wanted* to do this.

"Those of you who know me well will know that I spent time in the early part of my career in South America, specifically in Chile in the mid nineteen seventies."

"It was not a good time to be in Santiago. It was the time of *Plan Cóndor*, of a level of state terrorism, of cruelty enacted by one section of the population against another, that I can now scarcely believe. It hung like a miasma over the city. There was a man I knew by sight, he held the keys to some of the University buildings, kept things tidy, a kind of caretaker. I came in to the library one morning and found him sitting at the edge of the car park, covered in blood. He told me that that morning two soldiers had kicked in the door of his brother's apartment and killed him in his bed with the butts of their rifles. This man, he had peered around the door jamb and seen the aftermath of it, a river of blood, and the soldiers laughing, wiping it from their guns and boots, one of them lighting a cigarette. He had run, but only as far as his work. There was nowhere for him to go, and by that afternoon he expected to be disappeared himself, to end up on a rubbish dump somewhere in Argentina. I offered him money, and he looked at me as if I might be insane or on fire. In his eyes, to be seen associating with him in any way might be enough to have me disappeared too. He smelled of blood and desperation, and to me the whole city seemed to smell that way, and those soldier's boots and gun butts hovered in the sky above it.

I was at the end of a six-month student visa, based at the *Universidad Técnica del Estado*, rooming next to a post-doctoral American called Asther - Martin Asther. There were hardly any foreign students left by that time, and I was reasonably sure that at least two of them were DINA – secret police, or spies. I was collecting street mythology, taping urban folklore for my first post-doctoral papers. These would eventually become *Fear, Power and the Modern Totem*. It was an extraordinary time. Winter was coming on and fear came with it. Fear makes things very bright, invests them with a terrible intensity, and I was twenty-eight years old and surrounded by young people who felt the fear but had such vivacity, such strength..."

He spoke the last four words in a halting

papery whisper that embodied his grief at the altered circumstance that time and a failing body had brought him; the absurd calamity that his life had become. It should have been impossible to listen to, the grief of a dying man, but for me there was something in Noble's manner that made it bearable, the control of storytelling, perhaps, or perhaps a sense that he was acting. Effective teachers are almost always good actors, and my drunken mind liked this fuzzy notion - that Noble's tone and manner brought with them the detachment of the lecture theatre, the cunning of a motive as yet unseen. My perceptions may have been blunted by the wine, though, since I saw several Dons shoot satisfyingly disgusted glances at Jardine.

"...and I was in love, in a way. In the spring I had been visiting a family in the south of the city; they were distant relatives of someone I had known at the college, so I had an introduction. The eldest daughter of the family certainly caught my eye and I pursued her half-heartedly for weeks. I must admit that she was... She had a quick, sure way of moving... of moving her hands, or of tilting her face."

With his eyes half-lidded Noble's lean face echoed the movement he had seen long ago.

"Anyway, she was very striking, and as it grew colder, as things worsened in the city and my academic work stuttered to an end, it seemed to me that she and the city became the same thing: hunted, as if she had been marked long before by some terror which had waited, and now moved towards her, slowly but surely. She had no interest in me, and put me off with flattering mockery at first, and later with some irritation. As far as she was concerned I was a tourist, unable to understand her country's situation, to understand *her* situation. In fact, as the disappearances began in earnest she came to regard me with the contempt of one who is drowning, and sees another on the shore calmly discussing the weather. When I asked her to come to England with me, to marry me, her contempt deepened to the point where she spat at me on the street, cursed me, and wished that I had never been born."

"As it happens she was right to regard me with some suspicion. Asther was always very vague about his personal background, but razor sharp about his academic credentials and exactly who he had worked with and where. It made me suspicious of him, and I didn't like him much. After a few drinks I poked around in his room one day, and found a box under his bed which contained about five thousand American dollars, a list of names and addresses, and a small pile of mimeographed magazines entitled *La Libertad del Trabajador* – Worker's Freedom. It was an underground communist pamphlet, a little eight-page smudged thing in purple ink. I recognised some of the names, and I think Asther was an assassin of sorts. He would visit these names and addresses in the city, stuff a copy of *La Libertad* under the front door, or poke it through a window, or leave it under the mat. Sometime later, the security forces would discover this dangerous reading matter and the person in question would be dragged off for internment and probably a horrible bloody death somewhere.

I wondered exactly how hard the Foreign Office would rattle the sabre for me if *my* name were to appear on Asther's list, but that seemed a remote possibility to me, and I would be leaving soon.

The day before I was due to fly back to London I was sitting in the Cousiño Park, saying goodbye to the city I suppose, and Sofia approached me. It was dusk, almost curfew, and there was hardly a person around and so she surprised me, coming out of the gloom of the hedgerow and sitting beside me, and it was odd because she was how she had been before, way back in the spring of seventy-three, in September maybe, not in that cold and bloody July. She was wearing a white dress, and oddly, she was barefoot. I was frightened for her and asked her if she was not worried. She could be picked up by the DINA for any small thing and that would be that, but she just gave me the most beatific smile I have ever seen. She was sunny and glad and answered my questions only in the most oblique ways. She asked me enthusiastically about London, and then about Oxford – what was it like, how the people behaved there, how they dressed, and I began to have a sense of déjà vu, as if I were sitting alone reliving a memory, not speaking to her in the twilight.

We walked, and she stayed on the grass because it was soft on her feet. At one point she reached out to touch my hand, as if we might walk, hand in hand, but somehow our palms did not meet. I almost told her of what I had seen in Asther's things, that her name, her address appeared there in his latest list. She explained to me gently and firmly why she had rebuffed my proposal to take her away to England (more than she had done when I made the proposal the month before – then it had been all screams) and somehow I said nothing. I was flying tomorrow, leaving this awful place. She could not go to England with me, she said, because I was spoiled and uncomprehending and perhaps a little dangerous. *Peligroso* - I think that means somewhat dangerous. Finally, she asked me to forgive her, and I thought she meant for the mild insults she had offered and so said yes, of course.

'It grows colder.' She said, as we parted, one small hand held out slightly, palm towards the grass. The corners of her mouth had turned upwards in an odd smile that made me stand still and look at her carefully. It might have been mistaken for wistful, her expression, but suddenly I found it vulpine.

'It's cold. As winter comes I am stronger.'

'What is that? Neruda?'

A light rill of musical laughter.

'It is the truth. I cannot explain it to you. You won't know it until you are me.'

A panic I could not then explain rose up in me. It was the need for preservation. At the time I tried to pretend that there was some remorse in me. That I was sorry for what I had not said, not done, and wished to preserve *her* to save *her* from disappearance. Now I know that it was simple self-preservation. Some part of me sensed an inexorable danger, that I tiptoed at the crumbling edge of a chasm so deep that its floor could not be seen. Her breath in the darkness there was the breeze of some impossibly long fall waiting beneath my next step.

'Come in with me. Don't go home. We can go straight to the embassy, ask for asylum. I can get you out.'

The smile remained as she shook her head, then faded away from me into the darkness.

'I am already out.'

It was her smile that stayed with me as I did my evening things in my room, an almost monastic routine. It would not leave me, and I felt that at any time I might turn and see her by the door, or sitting on the slatted bed holding her knees, offering it to me for interpretation. My unease grew steadily over the evening. I had a bottle of rum, and I drank more than I should have. It did not relax me, but instead made me feel a lack of control. A sober kernel of me observed my behaviour with mild amazement as I displayed every nervous tic and self-comforting gesture I have ever learned. I paced and stretched and the muscles in my thighs grew weary because whenever I sat I bumped my foot up and down in rhythm with my pulse. I wedged a chair under the handle of my door and even stuffed a shirt into the gap at its bottom, so that no death card magazine might be shoved under, then searched my belongings, as if my unease might be a premonition of my own downfall. I moved the wardrobes and slit the mattress cover and rehearsed my journey to the airport and onto a plane to London over and over, then finally slept sprawled on a ruined bed."

Here Noble paused to lean forwards to grasp his own drink and lift it to his lips. Around him there was respectful silence. He closed his eyes as if mentally rehearsing, or perhaps re-living the next section of his story, then replaced his water glass on its tray and with his right hand slid the cufflink clasp from the buttonhole by his left wrist out of its housing and placed it also on the tray. Methodically, he rolled his shirt in neat folds almost to his elbow. My admiration for the man grew. It was a bit of stage business, an unhurried tension-builder that would have pleased the most talented of actors.

"In my drunken sleep I felt myself moved by a crowd of people whose faces I could not see; they were clouded, far away. I felt shoulders at my shoulder and an undeniable motion carrying me towards some fate I wished to avoid. Then close to me there was a scream. This was not like the screams that I had heard in films, or on TV, which are cartoons of screams, an outline only, but a real cry of fear and pain, an involuntary thing, wrenched out, more frightening because it provoked instant empathy, an unwelcome and immediate understanding of the extremity of the situation that would provoke such a sound. It died into a thick-sounding despairing moan, and though it could have lasted no more than ten seconds I found myself giddy with gladness that it was over and not currently in my ears.

I opened my eyes to my room, dark and still and quiet. My bedside clock said three-twenty AM. I blinked stupidly. My door was open, perhaps an inch, so that I could see faint light from the hallway glinting on the brass tongue of the lock. The chair I had wedged under its handle lay in the centre of the room, placed neatly and squarely on its feet, the shirt I had stuffed in the gap under the door was draped across its back.

I drew myself up onto one elbow, wondering again what the Foreign Office would do for me if I disappeared. Who would even report me missing to them? Could I expect any loyalty from Asther? Perhaps this was his doing – tidying up loose ends.

When Sofia padded into the room from my small kitchen I felt relief. She walked calmly to the very end of the bed and sat on its edge. From a distance I felt her weight on the old mattress, but she did not relax and let her weight settle; she perched there, as if ready to fly at any moment. She looked towards the centre of the room and her hair was loose and hung around the sides of her face, shielding her expression from my view.

'I've come here, because I want you,' she said. Her voice was small and monotone.

I shifted again, trying to throw off my confusion, still drunk; the chair, placed so carefully, kept attracting my attention.

'Are you alone?'

'Not now that I've come for you.'

Still no tone in her voice - no anger, certainly no desire, but there was something there, something hard and determined and perhaps a little mocking. She had changed from the last time I saw her and wore jeans and a cotton shirt, a light colour I could not identify in the gloom. A drop of some liquid fell from under that shield of hair and fell onto the fabric covering her knee. My eye was drawn to the droplet, the irregular spatter it made. Her right hand lay lightly curled before it, and in the half light I thought that it was a grey and ruined thing. The nails were missing from her index and ring finger, and a trickle of dark liquid ran steadily down the inside of her wrist and dropped onto the dusty floorboards of my room; I saw it and then heard it patter in the dust.

I became aware, through the fog of alcohol, that I was afraid. Not afraid in the way I had been on waking, afraid of the DINA, afraid of events to be dealt with, to be suffered through or overcome. This was a more visceral fear, a new thing to me. It was as quiet and stealthy as the cold of a winter evening which settles around you and chills you from skin to bones before you have realised that it has arrived. For the first time in my life I was afraid for something greater than my physical being, and as she began to turn towards me, to sit straight and regard me properly, I found myself consumed by the childish belief that if I closed my eyes tightly and could no longer see the scene before me - the gloomy room, the slight girl turning - that I would somehow return to my sleep and awake the next morning untroubled.

I did close my eyes, tightly enough for me to see galaxies of maroon and violet stars shooting across my field of vision and dying away into capillary red. There is a thing that scientists call 'dark sight', and it is the ability to sense objects, to feel their presence in an almost, but not quite, visual way. It is a sense that is plugged directly into some primordial part of the human brain, and with it I sensed a mass moving, and knew that she had moved and was now sitting directly before me, inches from my face.

'Coward. You could have stopped this.'

Her voice was still soft and almost expressionless, but her sentiment was devastating, in itself this was a perfect symbol for the stealthy thing that had come to my room in the middle of the night.

'I've come to you. Just as you dreamed I would.'

Of course - she was a dream; booze and sweaty guilt had conjured her and put her before me. She was an insubstantial fragment of me. When I woke in the morning this dream would be withered by distance and I would see its inconsistencies, its kinks and absurdities, plainly.

This revelation brought me such relief that I let out a pent-up breath. This was arrested again half-way as the dream-thing before me reached out and gently grasped my forearm with one slender hand.

I did not, or could not, open my eyes. Her hand was very cold; it was her right hand, as I could feel the nails of only three fingers prickling my flesh.

'You wanted caresses. This is my caress.'

Her grip on my arm tightened. Her fingers could reach only part way around and one after the other I felt her raise her fingers and dig the remaining nails into my arm. The pressure there increased steadily until I felt her talons pierce my skin.

'Three crescents,' she said; a mocking lover's whisper. I did not need dark-sight to tell me that she had leaned forwards to put her lips close to my face. I could smell sour sweat and decay.

'I mark you with a winter moon. It will bring me back to you.'

I felt intense pain in my arm where her nails pierced me and a sense of something imparted. My mind staggered and tried with limited success to represent the sensation for me. Things, images, raw images were dredged up from my past, my boyhood, and I saw then again, replayed. My first images of winter and death, my first comprehension that life had an end. A leaf, bruise-yellow curled over on itself, contorted like a wounded animal, then tumbled away by the wind. High stalks of grass by some ditch side, seen from the window of my father's Austin ten, leaning into a sky greyed by waiting snow. The fence of Winchester field, a ramshackle thing of logs bleached almost bone-white upon which someone had nailed the corpses of five moles in a line. Sad little ragged pelts and stiff pink feet, a country remedy, a bit of folk-magic to ward off pests, and I could feel my father's big hand in mine and the rough texture of his wool trousers, and that we had stopped our walk by this fence so that I could learn some silent lesson. These things were hard and cold and dismal."

Unbelievably, oily yellowish tears had sprung to Noble's eyes and run down his hollow cheeks. Dobrey leaned forwards and again put a comforting hand on his shoulder, mumbling something, but Noble ignored him and raised his arm, wrist outwards, and we could all clearly see that in the thin white flesh there, there were three crescents, looking like a moon becoming thinner as time wore on.

"Ghosts are not insubstantial things," he said at last, almost too quietly to hear. "They are not bits of cloud that come and go and might be blown away with a good lungful of air. They are real and solid, intruding into our world when they can, as solidly as anything else." He gestured around the room with his raised arm. "Look around you. Are the people you see here all real? Or do some of them cease when you no longer regard them. Are they *mechanisms,* things set up in one time to act upon another? Or do they think in the here and now? Make plans? What could they want?"

He seemed to draw back from some speculation.

"I know what Sofia wants. She died with me on her mind. Her betrayer. Someone standing in the sunlight whilst she was dragged off to some awful place for a sordid, undignified, painful end. Why she focussed on me rather than her tormentors, or Asther I don't know, but she did, and she has dogged me with pitilessness and with guile ever since."

He put his head in both hands so that thin strands of hair fell forwards before one naked and one clothed wrist, then looked up at Jardine, rubbed at his eyes, dragging away the oily tears, and settled himself.

"I returned to Oxford, outwardly normal. I married. We seemed to settle, but I never settled. I was haunted; she was always with me, and I saw things, heard things. She was toying with me. Four years after my return from South America my wife was involved in a car accident, a fatal one. When they pulled her from the wreck of her car she had one obvious injury: a large compression wound in the centre of her chest where her sternum had hit the steering column. She had swerved from the road to avoid something there, an animal the police thought. In the snow her brakes were ineffective and she hit a tree and suffered arterial damage that resulted in her bleeding to death before the first passers-by happened upon her. The police reckoned on two hours between the crash and discovery - two until four AM. The coroner said she would have been unconscious from the time of impact, and bled to the point of organ failure in about an hour and a half. I often pray that he was right and not just sparing my feelings, because I do not like to contemplate what she might have felt, or seen, if consciousness had returned to her.

I came to the Radcliffe to identify her, and they let me sit with her for a little while.

I remember the yellow sweater she was wearing; remembered seeing her pull it on with a crackle of static as she left out at lunchtime of that day, and I remember that someone had left a thick plastic bag, filled with her personal effects: purse, an earring, her coat, leaning neatly by the side of the gurney. I cried a lot, and took her hand and found that she also had several minor injuries. They were listed in the Coroner's report: 'minor contusions to right hand, including the loss of the fingernails of first and third finger, presumably as a result of high-speed impact with shattered polypropylene dashboard.'

I went to the Radcliffe car park, I needed a cigarette, and I can still remember the black and white pattern that the trees and streetlight made on the asphalt out there, a meaningless thing, a horrible desolate ideogram. I thought of her, the body I knew so well, pinned in that stupid car, and of a vague figure in the snow, barely a shadow, watching the impact and then, inexorably, approaching the wreckage.

In the cold, or *because* of the cold I was seized by a sense of *her* as always approaching, always becoming imminent, as existing in the fabric of my life now as surely as if she were information encoded into its DNA. She could materialise from the stuff of the asphalt, the light and shadow there, or the bulk of the building behind me at any point. A shift in the light and she would be close enough to touch me;

that is what it is to be haunted.

I stubbed out my cigarette and hurried back into the building, back to my dead wife, as if there was something there that I needed to protect, as if it wasn't already much too late. And there *was* comfort. It was better to be in that small grubby room with my wife's battered corpse than out in the world where *she* might be."

Perfect.

Noble buttoned up his shirt cuff in silence. I surveyed the room. There was some admiration that so late in his life Noble should try so hard to entertain us, for the strength of his character and the power of his voice. Some genuine grief that, whether real or a performance, Noble should be put to any discomfort. Some narrow interest at this reference to the circumstances of Noble's wife's death – a subject with a strong high-table taboo. Mostly, I saw the simple embarrassment due at any display of extreme emotion – real or conjured. Noble had *cried*. In fits and starts my gaze circled around the dim room and came back around to Jardine. It seemed to me now that his chair was a little farther out towards the centre of the room, a little more separate from those about to judge him.

It has to be said, he didn't help himself. On his face there was still a remnant of his idiot grin; perhaps he imagined that it was charming, but it looked like hard scorn.

"If all ghost stories were of that quality, Dr. Noble, then perhaps the form *might* survive, but I'm afraid they just aren't."

Further away from Jardine you would not have been able to judge Noble's stare, but I could see it, and his little blue eyes burned like hard pieces of starlight.

"To you, standing on the shore there, this is just a good story. Well I can change that Jardine," he said, a low-pitched, even tone. "Soon I will be dead."

Another hand on his shoulder-

"Morris! No you'll..."

He waved a quietening hand, a collection of long pointed fingers.

"Probably within weeks. You all know it. Pancreatic, Metastasised; hurts a lot... Anyway. Think about this, Dr. Jardine, because this is the essence of all good ghost stories. Soon I will die. And after it has happened, I will do everything, *everything* in my power to come back. For *you*."

A long pointing yellow-nailed finger; a cadaverous grin; then, by leaning backwards in his chair, he withdrew from the threat and regarded it like the rest of us.

"And if at some point during the next year *that* does not give you pause, then I bow to you Jardine, because you are the most rational and hard-headed man ever born."

With the punch line delivered, some tension seemed to bleed away from the room. So it was just a story; the whole thing the bad joke of a very sick man, and made at a junior's expense. Jardine stroked his chin. Those around Noble enclosed him in warm (but nervous) laughter, and he shone his horrible one-day-you-will-be-as-I grin around at them.

It seemed to me that all of the discomfort the little scene had generated had to go somewhere, and I could almost see it coming to rest on Jardine as each person in the room considered what they had heard and seen and where any left-over bad feeling should be deposited. Jardine felt it too, the court of the room, the room filled with people vital to the advancement of his career, finding against him. He was shrewd. Further abject apology would only increase the embarrassment. A show of aggression would be poorly received in the short term, but later? Surely it would be better to be remembered for a robust defence of his argument.

"If I may say, Dr. Noble, though effective, your story is full of holes. Why are all killers not haunted? Surely all murdered girls should return to haunt their killers, yet I am sure this does not happen. Why did your ghost wait so long to exact her revenge? And surely her real vengeance fell not on you, but on your wife. Also your ghost bears an uncanny resemblance to those hungry spirits you describe in *Fear and the Totem*," here his fool-grin widened, "almost as if you had borrowed a recurrent theme from the traditional beliefs outlined in your research and given it a personal twist."

Noble's bright gaze did not waver. "I cannot say why she, of all victims, was created, or why she did the things that she did. I have come to think of her as a remnant of the girl I knew in Santiago, a bit of sharpened will powered by hatred; such things cannot be judged by rational measures. Perhaps she waited until the time was right, or until she was strong. Perhaps for her no time had passed. Certainly, my wife paid with her life, but I have spent decades cowering under the guilt of it. I killed my wife with the cowardice that I displayed years before I met her. Cancer is biochemical, they tell me, but for me it is also spiritual, a final physical manifestation eating me alive. And yes, she was like some dark winter thing from a folk tale, but that should concern rather than comfort you, Jardine, because it suggests that each of us might receive the ghost that we deserve."

As the meeting broke up, and the college's great and good fled to their rooms or their homes, many still muttering over Jardine's insensitivity, these words seemed to me to linger in the softly lit college corridors and inform the term to come.

Two

That first winter was like a cruel stained-glass window with a flat cold light behind it. Though I worked hard to avoid him I met Jardine alone three times over the next several months, and each time remains as bright in my memory as a jewel. The first came three weeks after Noble's story. I was in the alleyway between the new and old buildings of the college. The clocks had gone back, British summertime was finally over, Halloween had passed in Oxford with its usual flare of costumed malevolence, and this was a white-skied November twilight, all misty breath and odd, flat illumination. I felt as if I were trapped between blond facets of stone, walking to my rooms, and then Jardine loomed out of the dimness, probably heading for his; he was unavoidable. I slowed and rubbed my hands together in the cold, hoping we would exchange some stupid pleasantry and leave each other alone - and so it was.

I nodded a curt hello, and he walked past me, shoulders hunched, hands thrust deep into his jacket pocket, then thought better of it and turned.

"I think you might have ruined me, Garrod,"

he said. Obvious anger mixed with an odd levity; I prepared to bluster and console and perhaps deny.

"Well done."

To that I found myself nodding again, unable not to take the plaudit. He seemed to have nothing more to say, so I began to back away from him and half turn.

A smile, or a showing of teeth at any rate.

"One should be careful whom one irritates, it seems."

I stared at his doughy face, thinking that this was certainly so, and he took my expression for incomprehension and made some gesture towards the old building, as if there might be an explanation for his words housed there, then he turned and hurried off towards his rooms.

In early December there was a surprise fall of snow and the city glowed under its pall. Walking up Broad Street it sparkled at my feet and softened the outlines of the Sheldonian theatre and the Bodleian. Before Radcliffe square I paused and looked up at the stone heads on pillars there, and it seemed to me that they were groaning under the cold weight. I saw them properly for the first time since my first weeks in the city and their heavy grimacing faces, scowling and pained, so pantomimish in the heat of summer, perturbed me, and I hurried into the shelter of the library.

When Christmas came it swept me up in red and gold. As full term ended the college gathered and gave thanks in chapel for its continued good fortune.

Many undergraduates and even some Dons found this overtly religious rite difficult to stomach, and in this godless age there were quite a few empty pews. Unsure of my beliefs I attended simply because I liked the communion of the hymns, the choristers red cassocks and ruffs, and the great arched windows of the chapel. It was time travel of a sort, as if the Victorian benefactors of the college, some of whom lay close by in the cold ground of the chapel yard, had pushed an imprint of their Christmas into the stones, and now we lived it through. The candles there burned as bright for me as the Christmas lights slung across Cornmarket, or those on the token tree I had put up in my rooms. In the first row, Noble's usual place was conspicuously empty. During the service and lesson I stopped listening and instead basked in the atmosphere: cold stone, wood polished to lustre by use, choristers kicking each other when they thought the choirmaster was not watching. A good celebration of the winter solstice, of *surviving* the winter solstice: the essence of Christmas. I had been seeing Ruth for a term or so, and we both planned to stay in college for the holidays and so this feeling would continue. I was filled with good cheer, a smile bloomed and I glanced around, wanting to share it and saw Jardine. He was sitting alone, eight or nine rows back, his big round zero of a face expressionless, lost in some private world. As I watched his hands came up above the edge of the pew, pressed together like a child's in prayer, and he closed his eyes tight and touched his fingers to his forehead. Clearly some private moment of pain or searching, so I looked away unwilling to meet his eyes when they opened.

At the very back of the chapel there was a wooden gallery, recently refurbished, and shadowed beneath it a funny little doorway which led eventually back into the college. A figure was slumped in the gloom there, in a wheelchair, watching proceedings amongst odd shapes of medical equipment - oxygen and suchlike. Noble, of course, the old way in had no steps for his chair to negotiate. His gaze was still bright, or perhaps I just remember it from that night in college. He was staring intently at Jardine, watching him from the cold corridor with what seemed to me to be hatred. We made a strange triangle. Jardine finished his prayer and looked up, saw me and followed my gaze over his shoulder to Noble. I was treated to the back of his head for what seemed a long time, then he rose and bobbed his way down the chapel to exchange a few words. Though I strained and struggled I could hear none of their whispered conversation.

A late bloomer and perhaps somewhat sheltered by the academic career I had chosen, I was then at the very tail end of adolescence. Full maturity beckoned, but independence still held a trace of novelty for me, and that Christmas in college with Ruth was one of the best I can remember. The early snow had melted, but it was, at least, cold, and for a week around Christmas day a sharp frost settled on the square of quad that we could see from my rooms and the sun did not reach it to burn it away. Ice formed and stayed on the redundant gaslight brackets at the stairway doors, used in summer to hang baskets of trailing plants. I could see candles glowing in some of the rooms opposite mine. The world glittered. We ate horrible microwave turkey dinners and my rooms were cold so we mounted a drunken giggling late night raid on Ruth's college to retrieve her duvet and her single-bar death-trap electric fire which, in the end, we were too scared to use.

Three weeks into Hilary term she would be off to Massachusetts for a stint at the Houghton library, combing through some obscure poet's letters, and this coming absence raised an unspoken awareness in us both that our relationship was more than a casual thing. We spent the New Year at my parents' house, and they liked her. All in all it was the last stretch of winter that I ever enjoyed and we sat in my parents' tiny living room and toasted the coming year with no sense of foreboding.

After Christmas things darkened. In some obscure way that I can still not explain when I waved Ruth away at Paddington, and the doors of the Heathrow express closed, putting a bar of reflected light across her distracted expression, there was a change, an ache, a pain that started so subtly and with such sly menace that it was only noticeable in retrospect. Whilst I sat in my warm and well-lit life, it was the beginnings of a vicious smile, the dawning of a notion of harm somewhere out in the darkness.

I taught and worked in the library day after day and ate my meals in hall. January closed with two tragedies. A Keble girl - some nondescript languages student in her second year – disappeared, and Oxford was flooded with Thames Valley Police, and after that, the press. There were appeals, and newspaper speculation, agonising mistaken sightings and re-hashes of several other undergraduate disappearances in the last three years. Finally, a macabre reconstruction of her last walk from Cornmarket towards her college was staged, but nothing came of it: she was never found. In the middle of this madness, one of my undergraduates was involved in a bicycle accident on South Parks Road. Someone opened the door of their car as she passed, and it catapulted her onto the road and into the path of another vehicle, killing her instantly. She used to write rather sharp and enjoyable essays, finely argued and intricate.

I gave her study partner a reading week and went to visit my sister. At first an unannounced house guest, disgorged dishevelled and wet from the train, made her grumpy, but soon she came to enjoy the sense of spectacle, of showing off her post-divorce success - her neat little house and well-organised family life - that I afforded her. When Nicky collected them from school I played with Owen, Evie and Julia. They were all under ten and still thought that visiting relatives, that any novelty, might be a treat. I watched the clockwork whir around me, and enjoyed seeing them be inside something. That week became their small house as night came on, the kids running about, yelling and playing hide-and-seek, and light and cooking steam leaking out through the kitchen window into the dark street.

I returned to news of Noble's death. He had not made it to February, getting paler and thinner and more pained. In college, Jardine's reputation had seemed to fade as Noble lost more weight and sharpened and became keen as a blade. By the time the old boy panted out his last breath in a side ward at the Radcliffe, grinning up at the stained tiles of the fake ceiling as his pain medication fought an unequal battle against the cancer raging in him, Jardine's application for the JRF had been roundly rejected; mine was still pending.

The funeral was all green and black, and it seemed to me that emerald shards lay in the grass at Noble's graveside, making patterns that were hard to follow. What strange thoughts would chase each other around a mind so disordered by terrible pain and powerful meds as Noble's, I wondered at that graveside, my live hands folded primly before me. As he himself had intimated, loves and hates, grudges and appetites would surely be sharpened like the shadows I could see around me, honed until they could pierce almost anything.

It was a humanist funeral, a cardboard coffin, but the Chaplain was there, looking oddly diminished in civilian clothing. The thing was well attended, both by college grandees and the wider academic community, but I saw no weeping family. Towards the end of the section where some people shared peculiarly upbeat memories of 'Morris', a woman in an ill-fitting plum-coloured suit stepped forwards, unhooking something from around her neck that glittered in the sunlight. As she passed me, I could see quite clearly that it was a small stone ankh held on a fine link gold chain. Completely silent, she tossed it into the grave where it made an unimpressive thock-clatter, then took a step back and tried to lose herself in the group there. Later, nursing a drink in the Norringham room, which the college had given over for the afternoon to receive those grieving for its favoured son, I heard her tell the Bursar that she and Noble were old friends, and that he had asked her to do it months before, because mourners needed something to gossip over, and 'what was a funeral without a little mystery, anyway.'

There was precious little mystery in the funeral leader's final speech. It lacked the terrible simplicity of 'ashes to ashes, dust to dust...', and was leant solemnity only by the bells of Merton and Magdalen chiming two. Part way in I glanced up and saw Jardine hovering on the outskirts of the graveside group opposite, darting behind a little troupe of fresh-faced undergrads who were all impressed by the solemnity of the occasion and their own forbearance at getting out of bed before eleven-thirty, so that he was out of sight of the college grandees. He bobbed there, ridiculous, cartoonish, his big round blank face like a balloon, showing here, then there over other people's heads.

He looked haggard to me, squinting because the sun was on my side of things, his thinning hair all sticking up on one side. He was a dull mote in my sight, scowling, wearing scuffed shoes and an unbuttoned anorak.

He left the service before me, flitting away so that he would not be noticed by anyone more senior. He caught up with me later, blind-siding me again as I lingered in the yard, coming out from behind the weathered parson's arch.

"Tell them what you did to me!"

He hissed it, and I thought I could smell alcohol on his breath. I glanced around us, relieved that only a few mourners had lingered to see this interchange.

"I don't know what you mean."

He bent slightly at the knees, and closed his eyes tightly, scrunching the lids together like a child preparing for a tantrum.

"Please go," a miserable whisper. "Leave me alone."

I took two steps away from him. His eyes opened again.

"Tell them what you've done to me Garrod, or I swear I'll..."

His threat trailed off. God help me I thought that he was still talking about the post in college, about a *job*. I thought back over our brief interchanges; there was nothing said there that he could possibly use against me, and somehow his lack of control increased mine. It disgusted me that he should be so easily bested, that he should fall apart so quickly, it was a species of incontinence.

"Tell what to whom?"

"The committee. That you did it to me."

Last year's leaves blew across my shoe-tops as I considered what he might mean.

"Go away Jardine," I said. "Go away."

The incident must have marked me, lodged in my mind as some kind of symbol, because a month later, as miserable February drew to a close, I dreamed of it.

My feet crunched on virgin snow, and below that a rime of ice that wanted to kick me off my feet and land me winded and bleeding. Around me I could see and sense the gravestones of the college boneyard, but the little yard had been stretched and warped by my sleeping mind so that it now covered miles of frozen land. Leaning grave markers stuck through the snow like snarling teeth. The college trees, grown impossible large, were black shapes out on the horizon; their branches twisted together, leafless, always coming to savage points. I felt afraid.

I walked for some interminable time whilst my mind impressed upon me again and again how the familiar comforting surroundings were altered, become untrustworthy, until, still far in the distance I could see the parson's arch and realised I was standing ten feet or so from Noble's graveside. I could hear a terrible cracking, splintering sound, like a dog working on a large milk-bone. I looked down at the grave, and where I thought there had been untouched snow I saw bloody footprints and two figures buried past their shoulders, locked in an intimate embrace by the earth. One rose slightly higher than the other, and was hunched over him at his back, almost capping his large head. As I watched, horrified, the higher, narrow figure leaned forwards, vulpine, and bit into the back of the lower, wider figure's head, tearing and gnawing. A step closer and I could see an oxygen tube snaking up from the earth into the higher figure's nose: it was Noble, gaunt and bloodied. As I watched he turned from his appalling meal and transfixed me with a feral stare.

"He put this hunger in me," he hissed, then dipped for another bite.

The bitten man was Jardine. Without speaking I expressed my horror; the terrible landscape shivered into hills, contorted into valleys, and then was still. Noble's yellow teeth were bloody, I saw them as he laughed and the laugh turned into a howl.

"Guilty as Ruggieri!" he cried.

Another convulsion and the landscape fell apart around me and became the dimness of my rooms. For a few seconds the terrible scene lay in the shadows there: tooth-like grave markers in the piles of books; the doglike angle of Noble's head in the sweep of the curtains.

Ruggieri. Ruggieri?

As the sweat on the back of my neck dried in the cold night air I Googled it, but before I could read my phone's explanation I had remembered the name. A particularly nasty bit of the *Inferno*. My mind had cast Jardine and Noble as Ruggieri and Ugolino. Traitors both, the former had imprisoned the latter in a tower of famine with his four sons. He watched all four of his children starve to death, and in the extremity of his own hunger resorted to cannibalism. Dante met them both frozen, as I had seen Noble and Jardine, into the soil of Hell.

He put this hunger in me...

I saw Noble's teeth again, and shivered, formlessly afraid in my own rooms for the first time since passing through adolescence.

I have found that action is often the best way to dispel fear, and I could think of only one thing to do to calm my mind after such an unsettling vision. A bit of simple folk-magic. I dressed quickly in yesterday's jeans and shirt and pulled my boots on over bare feet. Through the quad and the main gate and a sharp left past the library and I was opposite the chapel and rounding the corner into the chapel yard.

It was cold enough to take my breath. A stealthy, settling cold that glittered in the grass at my feet, that seemed with its silence and clarity to be a sly invitation; it would be death to me if I rested in it. If I stopped and lay down in the snow by the library wall and rested, the cold would anaesthetise me and my life would seep out of me as surely as blood would seep through a fatal wound. The first person through in the morning would find my stiff corpse with bluish skin and frost on its cheeks.

Still, the reality of each footstep helped sap the power of my nightmare. It was not miles of interminable marching between library and chapel, but a matter of five hundred yards, then a further five hundred to the graveside. The college trees were as they had always been: softened in age, providers of shade and solace. The boneyard was a safe and private place, a quaint cluster of ivied tombstone, a place where I had once seen a student production of Othello, using one of the older tombs, spread with a white sheet, for Desdemona's marriage bed.

The place of Noble's grave lay in a hollow of shadow and my night vision was compromised by the security lights shining from the outside of the library. I stopped my rapid walk as I thought I saw a deeper shadow. There: something solid but then seeming to flow and coalesce, growing and moving upwards, capped briefly by a white smudge that might have been a face. I had the urge to call out, and first Jardine and then Noble's names came to my mind and I had to swallow hard, strangely horrified by the notion of calling out a dead man's name in sight of his grave.

I stood in indecision; my need to act, to destroy my dream with bits of real world, real earth, real bark from the real trees, ebbing, and I was seized by the need, not felt since childhood, to simply close my eyes in the face of an unaccountable and irrational fear and wish myself away.

Instead I took a step forwards and followed it with another. Slowly Noble's grave came into clear view and there was no-one there; the only person buried there was the real Noble, horizontal in his horrible cardboard coffin.

Superstitious fear, I have found, can be fought effectively with wholly superstitious means, and I decided that I would carry my plan through and touch the earth of Noble's grave; to feel its dark, cold, and above all ordinary grittiness would sap all power from my nightmare.

When I finally arrived, ready to stick my fingers into the earth, I saw that someone *had* been there ahead of me. This side of the grave lacked frost in a round pattern that suggested a figure had squatted, or more probably knelt (watching? praying?) on this side of the grave and melted it away. At the centre of the grave mound, soon to be tamped over with sod, there were finger marks where someone else had sought to get this grave dirt under their fingernails. In my dream Jardine had been here, and in waking I was sure that his oddly angular body had knelt here and his hands, white and root-like, had made these marks.

Seeing the grave dirt disturbed brought home to me the strangeness of what I was doing, and how difficult it would be to explain. Some of the irrationality of my dream had seeped into my waking life, it seemed, and now I stood and backed away a pace.

Off to my left there was a faint noise: feet? Someone moving stealthily on the frosted grass, avoiding the gravel pathway. I cast about me but could see nothing, no movement anyway. The thought of Noble, just feet below me, his struggle over, his animus departed to wherever, decay and the tightening of skin and sinew stretching his mouth into a humourless grin came to me. Yes, these superstitious nocturnal visitations to his grave would have amused him greatly, would have proven his point to Jardine with a simple, physical eloquence. Not wishing to be part of his final joke any more, I departed.

Three

By mid-March this almost imperceptible shadow had left me; a hand that had begun to reach for me instead retreated, leaving my life with such stealth that I forgot it, forgot the feeling of it as we came around to the sun, as I began to live almost wholly in daylight again. My sureness that it had been Jardine at Noble's grave side never left me, and it became a part of my general awareness of his deterioration as the year wore on. I heard rumours that he had taken to sleeping away from the college, once being woken by a tourist asleep on a bench facing Christchurch meadow. I meditated on his lonely figure slumped there whilst the cows over the fence chewed under clouds made by their own breath and regarded him solemnly. Certainly I rarely saw him about the building. Worse, it was said that he had become unreliable, not turning up to teach his classes and leaving his students' papers unread. After a month of this the great Fletcher, puffed up by the enormous success of his latest book on Eliot, called Jardine to his office and grumpily fired him. Two of Jardine's students, both nervous finalists, came to me, and the extra money came in handy for my own plans.

Ruth returned at the end of Hilary term, coming back to me with the spring sunshine. I met her at the station. I watched her, distorted by successive grimy windows of the train, appearing and disappearing again and again, moving down the corridor, tired and struggling with her bags. She was here and gone, here and gone, and the idea crystallised in my mind that I could not have her out of my life. I was pleased to see her so wholeheartedly that it surprised me. I suppose some part of me felt as if I was following a well-worn track: establish career, find partner, set up house together, children, retirement to some ramshackle place in France or Cornwall, then death, and she was a smiling contradiction of that. My joy at seeing her proved that I was not simply going through the motions; I genuinely liked this girl.

Deeper down though, down where the earth is colder, I knew that I was pleased to see her because the wintertime had been so disconcerting, and she had little connection to that.

With my extra income I bought a pendant from Cooks in town - a tasteful Edwardian thing with rubies that I knew she would like. Towards the end of May we went back to the pub on the river close to Iffley, where we had spent several early dates, and I bagged a bench in the shade of a willow and we drank warm gin and tonic, and we talked and made plans, and all the while I could feel the square edges of the pendant box in my trouser pocket. This corner of the pub garden faced upstream, and from here I could look over Ruth's freckled shoulder and watch the sun, dipping below the trees on the far side of the river, taking away their detail, turning them from dusty green to black and stretching their shadows by increments towards us. A quarter of a mile upstream the river was crossed by a pretty stone bridge with a miniature colonnade from where you could follow a path to the lock itself, out of sight but audible as a constant hum of churning water. I planned to give the pendant to her there, and ask her to move in with me. From April to October the river path was prey to tourists, and some sauntered there now. At the centre of the bridge, at enough distance to make one human being almost indistinguishable from another, on the spot where I planned to slip the pendant from my pocket and offer it, a figure stood, seemingly watching me; the smudge of face was angled to suggest attention at any rate. I sat up a little straighter. Jardine was physically distinctive, strung together too loosely, uncoordinated somehow, and I felt certain that it was him. My expression must have darkened, as Ruth glanced over her shoulder, then back at me, her brows knitting into a question. The figure leaned forwards, perhaps for a better look; for an instant the sound of the weir grew louder, and then he faded backwards into the green/black shadows of the trees and was gone.

I found that of all things I did not want to meet Jardine that day and listen to his gibberish, and so I waited an extra drink before we moved off towards the bridge.

All went well. When Ruth opened the box from Cooks and laughed at my ridiculous formality and sunlight glinted on the pendant lying there, she seemed to release a golden few months in our lives. We abandoned our college rooms and let a small neat house to the east of the city where Ruth began the final stages of her thesis. A fortnight after we moved in I was called into Fletcher's office and told that my application for the college's Junior Research Fellowship had been successful. The college basked in the sunshine and I taught classes with the windows open and the early summer breeze came through and felt good on my forearms. In July I took two weeks off and we spent it on the south coast. The weather was unusually good and the world was hot sand and cool water; we grew tanned and happy. Back in Oxford the same sunshine warmed the back of my neck as I sat and graded papers and listened to the glimmering call of swifts massing to migrate, and all the while poor Noble's body mouldered in the boneyard beneath my window-sill and Jardine circled me, a far-out and forgotten winter planet; a fragment in a strange orbit.

Four

We have forgotten what winter time means.

Cosseted by central heating systems and cavity wall insulation, by supermarkets stocked year round with unimaginable plenty, people in the north now feel only an echo of its terror. Winter is freezing. Winter is famine. Winter is darkness. In early mediaeval England, winter was the time when, walking home from the fields through a wooded pass, you might glimpse the recent dead, struggled back from their graves into the living world in muddied cerements to stare at you with a glazed eye and hiss the fire of prophecy to you in riddles. Winter was the time when shortages bit; when isolated communities watched carefully as their meagre stores ran down too quickly and the spectre of cannibalism arose. Small bones: fingers, thighs, buried far away from the bounds of the churchyard, jointed and occasionally marked by teeth. Winter brought cold that could, and often did kill, cold that bit your flesh, gnawed at you with vapid determination, blackening fingers or toes which then putrefied and spread fatal infection to your shivering body. In winter corpses were discovered in their hovels, lips blue, flesh frozen hard as wood, hidden beneath the lie of shining, pristine, gently curving snow drifts.

Winter is death's triumph. Days die too quickly and the night is long. The foliage dies from the trees and rots on the ground beneath them, leaving them bare and sharp. All lushness leaves the land and sky, the earth freezes like stone, and those animals who can escape do so, leaving the woodlands quiet. People no longer migrate and instead wait in winter's path. Because of this there are more suicides, more deaths due to age or illness in the dark days of January than in any other month.

All of this, I felt as my next winter dawned. If you live in the north and it is wintertime step outside now in your shirtsleeves, leave your modern cocoon and stand in the cold until it numbs you, and perhaps the race memory will rise in you also, those winter dead will call to you, and as I did, you will feel the echo of their dread and their desperation: winter's power - a destructive animus ready to be harnessed.

Five

    The night Jardine died marked the arrival of the next winter for me. An unusually damp autumn had flared in the trees and been wiped out by unrelenting freezing rain. The days were grey liars. On the threshold of your door you would expect them to be wet but reasonably warm; instead a hard chill seemed to have settled into the earth early, and the ground itself radiated this cold upwards. This chill had settled in me also, and as the days grew relentlessly shorter, unease stirred in me, and I found myself marked by the peculiar feeling that I was looking out for someone who was coming to me, perhaps with unwelcome news; that I was trying to glimpse a still figure on the horizon, or make out a face in the crowd so that they might be avoided. This was a background sensation, impossible to analyse at the time. I began to wake in the night, starting in the darkness and coming to consciousness with my eyes already open and staring, seeking something out. On these nights I would leave Ruth sleeping in our warm bed and pace the still unfamiliar house and check that the windows were locked and the front door bolted

In late November - mid-way between the festivals of Halloween and Christmas - these feelings came to a head. On Fridays I had no teaching load and I would commonly spend the mornings in the library and then work until the early evening at home. Ruth had various in-college commitments and preferred to work there, arriving home some time after eight. Changes of mood for me are rarely sudden, but they can be suddenly recognised, and as I stood on the doorstep, fumbling in my pocket for my keys on that grey afternoon, I felt an unaccountable need to hurry, to get the key in the door, turn it, and have it locked again at my back. As my fingers touched the cold hard metal, this feeling moved from sub- to full consciousness. Its strength surprised me, and I forced my hand away from the cold metal of my keys and turned to face the dreary street. Grey sky, moving towards dark. Denuded trees poking at the bellies of the clouds. Lights on in a few of the houses making a weak yellow glow, and that chill, numbing my face and fingers. There was no-one following me, no hunched figure ready to rob me, no snarling dog ready to bite me, and yet, clearly, I was afraid. This ordinary domestic scene appalled me, and I found myself ridiculously drawn to the houses where light spilled out across the lawns and imagined knocking at the closest door and asking, like a lost child, to be let in.

I was afraid; but of what?

As if he were at my side, I heard Noble's voice, grating with horrified realisation, say- *a shift in the light, and she would be close enough to touch me: that is what it is to be haunted.*

Absurd. With a shake of my head I dismissed the old man, and let myself in.

Once inside my actions were a parody of my usual Friday routine. I made coffee and found the kitchen to be too quiet. With the radio on, I found myself straining to hear something beneath its chatter. I set out work on my desk but was incapable of concentration, turning always to the closed door as if at some moment I would see the handle turn and it would be pushed open by persons unknown. I spoke to myself, for reassurance I suppose, and did not like the weak sound of my own voice. By four o'clock it had begun to sleet, dirty snow falling in straight lines, lacking its usual fluttering grace. At full dark I went from room to room and drew all of the curtains, making sure to switch the lights on first so that I would at no point be left in darkness. With the TV volume low I stared at the news, then a magazine show. As with the radio I felt as if this chatter might be covering some sly, but vital sound, and several times I muted the sound and listened. A noise in the hallway? Upstairs? I rose to investigate, but my traitorous mind provided me with an image of something waiting there, some distorted effect of a creature, pale and elongated, and I sat down again. I began to understand what Noble had meant about the terror of imminence, of a thing waiting.

I glanced at the clock with absurd regularity, wishing the hands would speed up, ridding me of the time remaining until eight-thirty when Ruth would arrive home and dispel this peculiar enchantment.

Just before eight someone knocked on the front door. I do not mean that someone used the ornamental brass knocker, or rapped with the edge of the letterbox as the postman sometimes did; but someone pounded on the door with a fist, hard enough to rattle it in its frame. This was certainly not an hallucination because I both heard and saw it; the house was small enough for me to lean outwards from my perch on the sofa and see the door at the end of the short hallway jumping in its frame. In the time it took for four or five knocks to land, my mind ran through a series of fevered speculations and tried out the accompanying emotional responses. It was a neighbour knocking with some distress or anger to report. It was Ruth, come early and going through the same doorstep anxiety that I had experienced earlier. It was two sorrowful policemen, come to inform me of some horrible news: Ruth, or my parents involved in an accident. Lastly, it occurred to me that if I were stood on the doorstep I probably could not hit the door hard enough to make it jump in its frame in quite that way, and from there my mind jumped to Jardine. Peculiar Jardine, whom I had somehow ruined, come to have it out on my doorstep. The knocking stopped and the hall was silent. I found it difficult to rise from the sofa, and did so only when I had taken my phone from my pocket, as if it might be an anchor to some state of safety.

The door was equipped with a spy-hole, and

I bent to look through it, squinting. It showed a distorted but bland view of the empty storm porch: bricks rising in even rows, an empty pathway and lawn brightened by a dusting of sleet which blunted its contours and was freezing into a rime of ice. By the side of the door was a brick-built storage area for lawnmowers or strollers and suchlike. If you positioned yourself carefully by the wall there, you could probably be out of sight from the door but within an arm's length of it. Blinking in the faint hope of a better view I shifted from side to side and thought I could see, or perhaps sense, someone standing there, a bulk, deliberately out of sight.

"Who's there?"

Meant to sound strong, a territorial challenge, but instead holding a note of weakness, a childish 'please don't tease me, I can't take it' edge.

Silence, but not, I thought, absence; there was something mocking in the nature of that quiet. I shifted again, trying to change the angle of my view, and thought that I saw movement.

"Who is there?"

Who indeed. But I sounded stronger this time, and as if the impetus in my own voice spurred me on, giving me a shred of anger to work with, I drew the chain back on the door and pulled it open.

No one there.

The cold hit me immediately, making me draw in a breath and clench my jaw. The street was as it had been earlier, except curtains were drawn. The streetlights reflected on the forming ice, giving the scene an odd glow, and there were a set of footprints in the sleet at the edge of my lawn. Not mine; I had used the path.

Somehow this tangible evidence of someone messing around kindled my ersatz anger into the real thing and I strode out into the garden. It was as I thought: a mess of prints by the storage area door, leading off down the sideway towards the long, narrow back garden. There was an umbrella on the table by the door, a compact thing, but made of stainless steel and comfortingly solid in the hand. I grabbed it, holding the handle tight enough to make my knuckles white, and followed the prints.

They did not lengthen, I noticed. Whomever had travelled down the sideway and into the back garden had not hurried, but kept the same steady pace, and one print – the left – was for some reason narrower and shorter than the right. I followed the prints into the darkness and emerged in the back garden to see, halfway along its length, perhaps twenty feet from me, a tall figure standing and looking out towards the back fence and the fields beyond.

The awkward stance was unmistakeable: one shoulder dipped low the hand turned outwards, one leg straight, one knee slightly bent, limbs somehow poorly strung together. I had guessed right; it was Jardine. He was strangely dressed, with a dark coat hanging from one shoulder and the sleeves hanging below his hands, covering them. He wore baggy track trousers, grey and shapeless, and only one training shoe. Bizarrely, my afternoon now made sense to me. Somehow I had known that he was coming.

"Jardine, what are you doing?"

My question caused him to turn, slowly, as if I were dragging his attention away from something vital, and as his face came around my anger and fear were tinged with concern. My impression was no doubt helped by the weird light in the garden, an unforgiving glow made as the ambient light reflected upwards from the frozen sleet; he looked awful. His skin was pallid, almost blue under thin irregular stubble, darkened and bruised to purple beneath his eyes, which seemed to have receded to the point where they barely threw back the glint of a reflection. His thin hair corkscrewed upwards above his ears in odd clownish points, as if he had just awoken. His mouth hung open, and I began to wonder whether he might be medicated, some heavy antidepressant or anti-psychotic might cause such a look.

"Jardine," I tried again, "What are you? Where's your shoe?" An absurd detail to seize upon, but it seemed to me to sum up the situation.

Jardine considered this, and I watched, fascinated, as a line of drool crept from the edge of his lip and ran down into the snow.

"Got you," he said. I heard it clearly, but his voice was a grating whisper. His vapid expression did not change, and yet something about him, his stance perhaps, or perhaps that tiny glint of reflected light in his eyes suggested a deep and satisfied amusement.

"It's like he said. He got me. Now I've got you. And then you will *be* me."

A statement of some fact I did not comprehend. It was spoken in a monotone, and was as devoid of humanity as the rushing of the wind in the trees.

"Why are you here?"

Silence; his arms swung slightly above the snow, then a cry and sudden movement. His mouth widened, exposing teeth. Rage in it, full-throated and awful, the noise you might make when fighting for your life, shocking in the still night. He charged at me, a loping run of surprising speed. I had a confused impression of those coat sleeves flapping in the air like the untied ends of a straightjacket, and the mouth not closing but staying wide open, ready to bite, to consume, and then he hit me hard with one bony shoulder and dumped me on my back in the sleet. It was shockingly cold, coming over my collar and onto my skin. Expecting further attack I covered my head with my hands, but it did not come.

No sound; no movement. Slowly I took my arms away from my face. I was breathing hard, quick panicky breaths that sent little clouds up into the night sky. The garden was silent but for my breathing. Had he gone? I lay seemingly frozen, not thinking, just watching those little clouds until a new fall of snow began. Startlingly white flakes were born in the darkness, as if made there from nothing, and then fell towards me in almost straight lines, adhering to a pattern of such beauty and complexity that I could not grasp it. I could hear it falling, like a steady drip, and when snow fell into my face it broke the spell and I rose awkwardly to my feet. The garden was empty, footprints in the thin snow and that odd light. Slowly I went to the edge of the house and looked into the sideway, expecting a hunched figure waiting there, but it was empty. I took it at a run and when the front door was once again locked behind me I began to feel angry again. I thought of all of the times I had seen Jardine recently, and realised that he had been stalking me. I saw an image of myself, cowering in the snow in my own back yard, and felt enraged. There was a dog-eared college directory on the shelf over the phone and I found the number for his rooms and dialled it. It was a re-direction that got me the voicemail of his mobile service and this made me bold. I told him to fuck off and never come near me again. I called him a psychopath and told him that after speaking to him I was going to call the police.

When it came to it some residual guilt crept in and stopped me. Instead I found Dobrey, the Bursar's number and dialled that. I gave him a lightly edited version of what had happened.

"He was in your *garden*?"

"Yeah. Screamed at me and pushed me to the ground. I thought he was going to," I almost said 'bite me', but then steered away from it, "really attack me."

"Did you call the police?"

"No. He looked awful. Unshaven, and he was only wearing one shoe."

"Oh God. This has been coming for a while. Since Fletcher fired him from teaching. I mean, he's always been an odd one, and he has some pretty stiff competition here; but he's clearly spiralled out of control and he's our problem until the end of the year when his funding runs out. This is clearly a breakdown..."

His voice faded slightly as he moved away from the phone to get something, a pen perhaps, then came back again.

"*Are* you going to call the police? Better for the college if you don't."

I hesitated, then thought of my own position, Dobrey was no-one to upset. "No. Of course not. But I will if he shows up again."

"Right. Right. Look, I'll try and track him down. If he does show up there, will you call me back on this number, so I can get involved? Easier to manage things when you have the whole picture."

Headlights washed across the front of the house, Ruth arriving home at last, and so I agreed hastily, wanting to go out and meet her.

I am suddenly awake, lying on my back just as I had lain in the snow. I wake with my eyes already open, adjusted to the dimness of the room and this gives me the impression that some great and shocking noise has thrown me from sleep, as if every item of furniture there had leaped into the air and crashed down around me. Ruth is still asleep beside me. Slightly nasal but calmly drawn and released breaths, tidal somehow, tell me that any alarm occurred only in my own head. I listen anyway, wondering if I might hear a stealthy sound instead: a light tread on the stair, the brush of fingers on the outside of the door handle. No. No-one is in the house but Ruth and me. Before sleep I had paced every inch of the place, and then checked that all of the doors and windows were bolted. Ruth had watched me do it with a carefully neutral expression.

Routine is the answer for these fears, and I had awoken in such a way so often during the autumn that one had been established. I rose slowly and moved to the door, avoiding the squeaky floorboard there, then once out in the hallway I turned on the light.

Downstairs I made tea, and rinsing my cup at the sink, stared out at the street through a chink in the blinds and felt calmed by its mundanity. After a few hours sleep the events of the early evening seemed remote and other-worldly. My nervousness in the house, Jardine in the garden - it all seemed like something an acquaintance might have told me about; something envisaged rather than experienced.

My phone lay on the counter. The lock-screen reported that I had email and muscle memory guided my finger through its combination though my vision was still fogged by sleep.

It was second from top, the subject line just a single full-stop, something from PAJardine@gmail.co.uk had arrived at one fifteen AM;

it was now a little after three. Its effect was as sudden and surprising as a dash of cold water. I stopped in the centre of the small neat kitchen where fluorescent light caught the edges of mugs and the stainless steel colander I had watched Ruth wash up hours before. I even glanced over my shoulder, as if the man himself might have appeared behind me; those ridiculous coat sleeved dangling above the clean lino.

I'm stupid enough to have no malware protection on my phone, so did not open it there; instead I went through to the living room and woke up my laptop.

The welcome tone sounded ridiculously loud, and made me reach for the volume control. It was an email with no subject, the digital equivalent of an unattended bag ticking in a train station. My finger hovered over delete, but instead I scanned it, got the comforting green tick then opened it. Empty, no subject, no text; it took me a while to notice the attachment. I scanned it and it was also apparently safe, and so I opened it.

Video. It unfolded across my fabulously vibrant display. A muddy brown image, scarred breeze-blocks: walls somewhere? It was badly lit, a clear sight of a line of cement, then a nauseating swing to a patch of concrete flooring, a jump cut and then Jardine, in the centre of the frame, leaning at an odd angle against the wall. He filled the image to the shoulders, and he was as I had seen him earlier, the coat shrugged from his shoulders, his face, in close up, shockingly pale, almost corpse-like. I had visited an uncle in hospital immediately after a heart attack, and he had had this colouring - doughy grey, purplish blue beneath the eyes, as if death had reached out and already taken something vital from him.

Jardine's lips moved. He was muttering, and it took me a couple of seconds to reach for the volume again and turn it up loud enough to hear him, so I came in mid-sentence:

" ...watched you, Garrod, that night. From the dark. Just like he watched me; a chain of us. We both had the same urge. Call answered. The dirt was under my nails for weeks..."

All spoken almost under his breath and very quickly, like he was speaking between painful breaths; an almost hypnotic drone.

"It's cold here. I feel cold and that's part of it, isn't it? Like he said. Cold's part of it, and it gets *in* you. You let something out and it comes in and you're different and I can feel it happening. It's happening to me."

His head lolled forwards treating me to a blurry view of his matted and corkscrewed hair, and then he looked up again and was smiling. No friendliness in it though, a simple retraction of the lips to show the teeth, like the snarl of an animal, whilst his eyes showed a feral cunning.

"I'm glad that we worked together," he said, more slowly and deliberately, "I'm glad that you could help me on my project."

Then, again, he speeded up.

"He was right. Because I'd never seen it, I thought... Tech's no help. Not when it is *real*. Haunting means everywhere, and you have to have people to call anyway, don't you? People to make it ridiculous. But if it's not ridiculous. You have to... It doesn't change what's in *here*." And he lifted one hand and tapped his palm solidly against the side of his head, his coat sleeve flapped. He looked out of shot, as if looking at something behind the camera or phone or whatever he was filming on, and, more shocking than his appearance or his rambling speech, began to cry.

"He's *here*." A whine, a noise that a dog might make as a plea for mercy, and much quicker breathing.

"Oh God. He's here."

A hand came up, shaking, the loose sleeve falling away, to cover his eyes; an act of denial, a refusal to see. He sat that way for a few seconds, and it seemed to me that there was a change in the shadows around him, as if the camera or the light source had shifted, or there was someone else moving in the room.

When his hand fell away I could see that it had left a viscous smear across his pale face. In the poor light it was a deep muddy brown, somehow lustrous and jealous of the light that fell upon it. I blinked and moved closer to my screen. Blood; that could be blood.

His sobbing continued, hitching through his speech, giving it an odd compelling rhythm.

"You did this to me. It hu-urts. I Ha-ate you Garrod. I read that it wouldn't, that you pass out before the pain, but they lie-ed. It hurts. I can feel it, feel it draining away. I'm bleeding *away*. It's colder. It feels like winter. I'm down there."

He gestured to something out of shot. There was a small movement in his shoulders, and the shot widened. I could see dirty concrete floor, the block wall I had seen earlier, and Jardine slumped there. His feet were splayed and one training shoe had come off. His right hand, which held something that was controlling the camera, lay in his lap. His left had fallen down by his hip, palm upwards, the fingers splayed out like the legs of a dead spider. It lay in a large pool of that muddy brown liquid, and, with his coat sleeve pushed up slightly, I could see that his wrist was a ragged mess. I saw three cuts - wider and deeper copies of those on Noble's wrist.

His head came up, shaking slightly with what seemed an incredible effort, and he stared straight into the camera. His eyes were dark pools on which light lay, underlined by those terrible bruises. He began to pull in quick shallow breaths, almost panting, and spoke around them:

"When it ... comes out ... it hurts ... I'll ... see you."

Our land-line was in the hallway and I found myself backing towards it, as if his presence on the screen might be a danger to me.

As I reached it and my hand fell onto the cold plastic, two heavy knocks sounded at the front door. I turned to it slowly, experiencing true dread, expecting to see Jardine's pale form, elongated and distorted through the privacy glass, perhaps punctuated by a spatter of blood from his ruined wrist.

Instead I could see two distinct dark shadows crowding the doorway, apparently standing shoulder to shoulder. I had to wet my lips before I could speak.

"Who's there?"

Movement above me, and I looked up to see Ruth's face, puffy with sleep, staring at me resentfully, then, as she took in the situation, a little frightened.

"It's the police, Dr. Garrod."

I took two strides back into the living room and looked out through the curtains; a police car was parked across the gateway.

"What is it? Is he here?"

Silence for a moment, then-

"Could you open the door please Dr. Garrod, we'd like to speak to you."

I stood in the hallway, reluctant to open the door, to welcome in some new and frightening phase of my life, but Ruth moved on the stairs, coming down, wrapping on a robe.

I opened the door but left on the security chain, unable to shake the fear that Jardine was here somehow, that he had come here and was slyly waiting, ready to slip out of the darkness, bleeding, trailing his coat sleeves. Two constables stood on the doorstep, a crime show cliché, one man, one woman, carefully expressionless.

"Dr. Garrod?"

I nodded. "Is he here? Do you have him in custody?"

"Do we have who in custody?"

"Jardine."

They shared a long glance.

"We'd like you to come with us please Dr. Garrod."

From behind me Ruth spoke up.

"Why? What's happening?"

The woman officer responded.

"Dr. Jardine was found dead at his home this evening, Dr. Garrod, and we've been asked to come and collect you, so that you can come and give a statement, and informally answer a few questions."

"Questions about what?" Ruth asked.

"I'm afraid we really don't know that."

"Can't it wait until the morning?"

I shook my head dismissing the idea, then flapped my hand at the kitchen where, presumably, Jardine's suicide video was still playing.

"He taped it and sent it to me. I was just watching it... "

Another glance between the constables and the man stepped away from the doorstep and said something into his radio, waited for a response, then stepped back.

"As I say, at the moment, this is still informal, Dr. Garrod, but we would like your statement now, while events are still... fresh, and constable Foley will stay until someone comes to examine your computer."

Through the doorway I could see lights coming on across the street, curtains twitching, neighbours discussing what kind of trouble this visit might represent. The fact that the policewoman would stay at the house comforted me somehow, and I nodded.

I dressed quickly in yesterday's clothes and finger-combed my hair, feeling numb, and unable to get the image of Jardine, slumped against that wall, lying next to an expanding pool of his own blood, out of my mind. As if it were an after-image of a very bright light, each time I closed my eyes I saw him, his dirty corkscrew hair and vapid gaze.

I looked at myself in the bathroom mirror, pale and watchful under a ragged growth of stubble, and felt an unpleasant flare of guilt. Tired and frightened I looked a little like him.

I reached out towards the glass, my fingertips shaking slightly, as if to commune with the pale shape there, and caught some movement in the mirror from over my shoulder. I wheeled around, taking a step backwards towards the wall, but it was only Ruth, hugging her robe around her.

"His... the movie was still playing on your computer. Jesus Jack, it's horrible."

I nodded.

"Why did he send it to you?"

I shrugged.

"What do they want to ask you?"

"I don't know."

She heard something in my tone, some defensiveness under the shock, and her expression softened and she stepped towards me reaching out to touch my arm.

"Do you want me to come with you?"

"No. I'll be fine."

And I was. I got into the police car for a ride around the ring road, which was shining and unfamiliar, curling through a bright rime of ice and snow, then on through town. There was no traffic this early in the morning, and the journey became dreamlike: the low hum of the car's engine, an endless parade of pretty, monochrome scenes passing by the windows, white fields, trees hung with new snow. Magdalen glowed with reflected light on the High. Its gargoyles stared down at me like warnings as we waited at the traffic lights. A grotesque old man, his mouth drawn downwards in a bow of pain or fear, his hands, like Jardine's hands, up, covering his eyes, pitifully inadequate defence against some company too appalling to contemplate. A contorted face, screaming in fear and rage, whose elongated serpent tongue writhed out and over its head. A thing with a lion body, wings, and a human face, its gaze contemplative and greedy, jealous and hooded. They were spirits of air made stone, manifestations in the true sense of the word. For the first time I wondered what their nameless mediaeval sculptors had witnessed.

Eventually I found myself in a small office with an untidy desk that had chipped edges. The constable left the door open, and I watched officers coming and going, alone or in pairs, hurrying or dawdling, and I envied them their matter-of-factness and wished that I was like them and passing through another unremarkable day. Half an hour passed, enough time for me to get restless, and I found myself pacing the office, looking at the calendar on the magnolia wall, pausing by the desk to see if any of the paperwork was readable. There was nothing but a notepad with a bullet-point list on it, inscribed in a small slanting hand. The top three points were illegible apart from their number, and I wondered if they were written in shorthand. Points four to six read: 4. Relationship/Animosity? 5. J. T.O.D./ Conflict. 6. 'you did this to me'?

As I read the last and traced the words with my fingertips I heard it spoken in Jardine's rasping monotonous voice. Once, then again, with a horrible urgency. I saw his chapped blueing lips move. Again I saw his hand rise and cover his eyes, leaving that awful bloody print, and I shuddered, feeling that I was being watched, observed somehow. The feeling was strong enough to make me straighten and turn towards the door.

A man was standing, just beyond its threshold, holding two paper cups of coffee. His pose was relaxed and static, as if he had been standing there for some moments, observing me. On seeing me look up he offered a faint smile, which I did not believe was for my benefit, and moved into the room, closing the door with one practised sweep of his foot.

"Dr. Garrod? Detective Inspector Hopper. Please have a seat." He put the cups down on the desk where they steamed, and marshalled his notes, looking at something in a buff folder, and then consulting the notepad I had read.

"Just a few questions before we get you to make a statement, if you don't mind." A glance at the notes-

"So you saw Peter Jardine yesterday evening?"

"Yes. He came to the house. He was disordered even then, raving. He knocked me down in the garden."

"Do you know what time this was?"

I thought about it. Ruth had arrived home whilst I was on the phone to Dobrey, so it must have been-

"About eight o'clock."

He nodded and made a note, not much more than a pencil stroke.

"Exactly what happened?"

"He knocked on my door, shouted at me and disappeared into the back garden. I followed him. He said some crazy things and ran at me. Knocked me on my back and ran off."

"And how do you know what the time was?"

"My partner arrived not long afterwards and she's usually home around eight-thirty."

"Do you remember what was on TV?"

"No. It wasn't on."

"Radio?"

"No."

"What time did you arrive home?"

"Close to four. It was almost dark."

He sat back in his chair and looked at me, balancing his yellow pencil between his fingertips. He had brown eyes of such deep colour that they were almost black, kindly under the right circumstances I suspected, but they regarded me with an open, almost hostile curiosity that I found disconcerting, as if I were a puzzle to be solved.

"What did you do then?"

"I called Dobrey at the college."

A glance into the buff folder.

"You called Marcus Dobrey, according to *his* records, at eight-twenty-seven. Dr. Jardine's voicemail service logged a call from you to him at eight twenty-one."

My call to Jardine, swearing, raving at him, calling a man on the point of taking his own life names. How had this neat, watchful policeman interpreted my words? There was nothing in his expression to give me a clue and suddenly tiredness seemed to overwhelm me. The light in Hopper's office seemed too bright, giving everything I saw an uncomfortable amount of detail. I saw each thread of the grey weave of his rumpled suit, every line in the grain of his desk, laid down by some unknown tree uncountable winters ago.

It was an effort to speak.

"If you knew the time, why did you ask me?"

The sharp look remained; I was being studied, my expressions and body language carefully assessed.

"Because I have a problem, Dr. Garrod. And it makes you either mistaken for some reason I cannot see, or a liar, which, since there is a dead man in the mix here, is a serious thing."

I rubbed my hand across my eyes and they felt sore.

"What do you mean?"

He leaned forwards, one elbow on his knee, and tapped on his pad with the end of his pencil to punctuate his sentences.

"We've worked out the time line like this. At three o'clock yesterday afternoon Dr. Jardine left the college library, after returning all of his books. He seems to have driven back to a property he owns to the north-west of the city which backs on to Wytham great wood and has two outbuildings - used to be barns, apparently. We don't know what he did over the next two hours, but by about six o'clock he was in position in the largest barn, sitting with his back against the wall with a digital camera on a tripod in front of him. The thing was hooked into the house's Wi-Fi network and takes a time signal from the internet, so we know he switched the camera on at six-twelve, by which point he already had what would be a fatal wound on his left wrist. This was inflicted in the kitchen with a carving knife, from the angle - almost certainly self-inflicted. He knew what he was doing. Made the cut up his wrist, rather than across so he didn't sever any tendons, and shallow enough to seep blood rather than gush, so he could control it with his other hand and have plenty of time to talk. He waited until he was close to the end, then some app on his laptop took the footage and emailed it out to us, and later on, to you. He lost consciousness in the film at about eight o'clock and is likely to have died a few minutes later. So you see that there is a problem with the timing. At pretty much the time that you say Jardine was in your garden," pointing at me with the pencil, "he was actually seven or eight miles away dying in a cowshed," pointing away. I stared, seeing Jardine's swaying figure in the low light of the garden, his hands and wrists covered by the sleeve of his coat.

"But he was there."

Hopper swung around to face me and placed the pencil on his desk.

"Assisting a suicide is a crime, Dr. Garrod."

I held his gaze.

"I came home by bus at four or so. Oxford bus company number three, I think. There will be CCTV footage from on board. I didn't leave my house until Jardine knocked, canvas my neighbours."

That fey smile again, and I realised that he had already thought of this, and tomorrow it would probably happen.

"How much of Dr. Jardine's video did you watch?"

"Enough. I don't know. A few minutes."

He reached down towards his desk, unlocked a drawer and took out a tablet. He typed in a code and the screen lit, then he laid it on the desk in front of me. It was playing the horror show I had seen earlier, framed by a series of rapidly changing figures, measuring out Jardine's death in tenths and hundredths of seconds. Even with no sound it was awful. I flinched away from his blue lips and bloodied skin.

"See that?"

I shook my head and he reached over and replayed the section of film. I recognised it; Jardine's hand came up to his eyes and left a bloody handprint on his face.

"He was sitting facing an open door. I was there earlier, and stood in that doorway. If the lights are on in the garden, standing there changes the quality of the light – like that."

He reached out and deftly scrolled the film back a couple of seconds, and he was right. The change there could be a figure blocking some ambient light.

Back to the folder, flicking through some pages:

"He says: 'He's here oh God he's here.' Any idea what he means, or who he means?"

Unbidden, an image of Noble rose in my mind, as he had been that night in college, cunning and cadaverous, grinning hungrily. It caused a fractional pause before my answer, long enough to tell Hopper that a name, or an image, or something

71

had come into my mind, but Noble had been dead for almost a year.

"No. Certainly not me."

"He says a lot of strange things in the video, doesn't he Dr. Garrod?"

"That's not surprising, is it? The man was *in extremis* and clearly deranged."

"Of course. But he sent the video to you for some reason, surely? He says: 'You did this to me, Garrod. I hate you.' And, 'he was right. Tech's no help. Not when it is *real*.' What does that mean to you?"

So I told him the whole sorry tale: that I set Jardine up that night in the Senior Common Room, that, as a queer joke, Noble had threatened him, that he had stalked me, and even that we had both visited Noble's grave on that winter's night.

When I finished Hopper was sitting back in his chair, playing with his pencil once again.

"Obviously, I didn't know how fragile he was. Noble couldn't have known what would happen, that he would take it seriously."

"Obviously." That evaluative gaze did not soften. "Did you go to the house at Wytham yesterday?"

"Of course not."

"Do you want to change *anything* about your story? Add anything?? Because I can't make these times square up, and as I said, that means you're either lying or mistaken, and I have to tell you Dr. Garrod that really bothers me."

Wearily I shook my head.

"I've told you exactly what happened. I can't explain the timing. Maybe he rigged his equipment somehow, I don't know."

"No. He didn't rig the equipment, he couldn't. Could you have lost consciousness when he hit you? Mistaken the time? Could it have been earlier than you thought when he came to the house?"

I saw mesmerising flakes of snow, born in the black sky, then falling down towards me. It was possible, he had seemed to disappear, but I had had no sense of lapsed time.

"I don't know."

He sighed.

"I'm going to have to send a forensic team to the farm house. Have you ever been there?"

I shook my head. He leaned towards me again, scrutinising me.

"Will you consent to giving a DNA sample?"

This time I did not hesitate.

"Of course."

Something in my expression seemed to satisfy him more than anything else I had said.

"Ok. We'll arrange that, but it's not like the TV. The chances of them finding anything of you there are one in a million anyway, not unless you licked the knife handle or sneezed on him as he lay dying. If they *do* find anything that I can link to you, we'll have to talk again."

He started to rise.

"I'll have someone come in and take you to where they can take a swab, and then an officer will take down and agree with you your formal statement."

At the door he turned.

"What was the project, by the way?"

My blank look forced him to explain. This time he did not look at his notes, he had committed the phrase to memory.

"He said: 'I'm glad that we worked together. I'm glad that you could help me on my project.' Was it a work thing?"

"No. I never worked with Jardine."

As if the cold of the night had somehow reached in through the police station walls and chilled me, I left two hours later, feeling numb. From the back seat of a taxi I saw the same scenes unfolding again, this time lit by the dawn. In the east the sky started clear, but the sun seemed to have no power, and as it rose a freezing mist rose with it, slyly shrouding trees and colleges so that they loomed out of the whiteness in fragments. With horrible inevitability we were caught in a queue of traffic by Magdalen again; and there were the gargoyles. I looked up into their stone eyes and they seemed to look back at me. I saw animal rage too great and bloody to be expressed in words but caught there in stone. I saw pity and regret and an appreciation of some horror yet to come. As I looked from stone face to stone face it seemed to me that I heard some sound, a roar or scream, both threat and warning and lament. It was loud enough to make me cower, but coming from a distance too great to measure. I shrank back from the cab window, and must have made some noise of distress, because the driver shifted in his seat to glance at me in the mirror. Again, I was seized by a sense of imminence, of something coming to me, at one moment slyly stalking, at another rushing towards me as Jardine had rushed towards me in the garden, and I was afraid.

At that moment, feeling the cold grain of the leather of the cab seat under the palm of my hand, a certainty arrived in my mind. I had not lost consciousness in the garden yesterday: Jardine had visited me after his death, just as Noble had visited him. *He got me. Now I've got you,* he had said. Like the Chilean girl in Noble's story, hatred and fear and pain had made some new birth possible for them.

Though it was nonsensical, absurd, perhaps only a result of weariness, nevertheless this was a belief as unshakeable in my mind as my belief in gravity or my expectation of the sunrise. What had Noble said: *a bit of sharpened will powered by hatred ... some dark winter thing from a folk tale.* Yes; I had been visited by some dark winter thing from a folk tale ... *cold's part of it ...* and I felt that as the winter drew on, it would likely gain in strength and come back.

Six

I began to understand something of what it must be like to live with some chronic pain: spinal arthritis, the middle stages of cancer, the aching of a phantom limb - something that was a constant squeezing, wrenching, grasping pain. The days that followed, followed a pattern I had established for myself: teaching, working in the library or at home, evenings and weekends with Ruth, and yet each day was stained by this pain, until it became familiar, not an external thing acting on me, but part of me. I saw it most clearly in the mirror. I looked tired, grey and worn down. I spoke less and thought more. I checked that the doors were locked in the house with ridiculous frequency and insisted that the TV or radio volume stayed low. I felt Ruth watching me carefully, quizzically at first, then with bewildered concern. During the day I resented her in the most cowardly way, she was safe and could not understand, and her concern felt like criticism. In bed at night we slept closer than we ever had, intertwined; I needed her warmth.

Two weeks after Jardine's death I came

awake in the darkness of our small bedroom. My eyes were open and adjusted to the gloom, but I had the sense that something had woken me, as if the sound of my name, whispered by lips that were inches from my ear, still echoed in my mind. I lay still, analysing the sounds around me. Out on the street, perhaps two or three roads away, a car was passing. Though she was turned away from me I could hear Ruth breathing; a tidal indraw and release. She was sleeping partly on my left arm, and as I withdrew it she murmured and turned and there was the whisper of fabric on skin.

Behind it all, I thought I could hear dripping, a very slow but absolutely regular drip somewhere inside the house, downstairs surely. I lay listening, unconsciously counting, and as if I were a child reaching a treasured goal, when my counting came to ten I swung my legs out of bed and went to the door, reaching for the handle.

My hand paused in mid-air, still reaching. Drip ... drip; definitely from downstairs. From here the sound was louder, and this was because the bedroom door was ajar. It yawned open from the jamb by three or four inches, offering a thin slice of darkened hallway: an invitation to the unknown. I looked down stupidly at my hand; I was certain that I had not left the door open, I never did. Ruth could not have come to the door without waking me; therefore someone else had opened it. I considered closing it, cutting off that terrible invitation and returning to the warmth of bed, but the thought that whatever had opened that door -the winter-thing, the shard of sharpened will- that it might become impatient, yet more angry, the thought of listening to it slowly dragging its steps up the short staircase to stand swaying by the door, was more than I could bear.

I was hypnotised by a symphony of tiny noises, Ruth breathing and on every third breath another drip, and I stood for a long moment examining the door handle as if it were a relic from another age. When I reached out to grasp it, my hand shook.

Walking down the stairs was difficult. I felt dread, true dread, which is an emotion with a strong physical component, flooding the body with adrenaline to chill the skin, tighten the muscles and narrow the mind's focus. I found that I had to force my feet to take each step, my hand to progress on the hand rail, as if some older, less evolved, less conscious part of me were trying to establish control and make me turn from my path.

Downstairs the hallway seemed too bright; reflections from the snow outside came in through the glass panels of the front door to put odd, jagged shadows on the wooden flooring. I walked over them, heedless of their sharp edges. At the door to the kitchen I was again faced by a triangle of darkness, again that terrible invitation. I stood there, waiting for my vision to adjust, and when it did I could see nothing out of the ordinary in that triangle of darkness: last night's tea things washed up on the drainer, Ruth's old trainers by the back door mat. Still that relentless drip ... drip sounded, and I was close enough now to localise the sound. Though we rarely ate in the kitchen there was a small dining set there in the far corner of the long room, out of sight from the doorway.

"Who's there?"

My own voice surprised me, a dry whisper in the darkness that I instantly regretted, because I knew that I did not wish to receive an answer.

Silence but for that steady, maddening drip plashing onto the tiled kitchen floor. An eloquent silence than unmanned me. I looked longingly over my shoulder at the front door. I could leave. The car keys were on their hook in the hallway. I could abandon Ruth and go to the college, to my parents' house, go to some random hotel somewhere where I was not known, but I suspected that wherever I went, I would soon come awake in the night to hear this same stealthy monotonous sound.

I pushed at the door and it moved with appalling slowness, tracking over the inches of flooring for hours. I followed its movement, stepped into the room and saw what some part of me had known I would see since I had come to consciousness in the bedroom.

One kitchen chair was pulled out from the table. They were old cottage things with ornate backs and curved arms. Jardine sat in the chair, slumped forwards slightly as he had in his terminal video. His head was forwards, his right hand, wrapped around the chair arm like a pale spider, his left arm dropped towards the kitchen floor. From his index finger, just visible below the hem of his sleeve, a large drop of blood was forming. As I watched, it reached some limit of weight and fell, joining others pooling on the floor: drip.

A sense of unreality washed over me. There was a dead man in my kitchen. For a moment I felt that I might faint, as if the world were withdrawing, becoming too far away. I fought against it, panicked at the thought of falling and lying helpless. Drip; and I saw the pale finger twitch and there was a slight movement in his shoulders, and without raising his head, he spoke, his voice grating and slow, barely audible:

"il traditor che io rodo."

Dante's Italian. My mind translated: 'the traitor whom I gnaw.' An image from my dream of last winter came back. Jardine, his head buried in the soil of Noble's grave, Noble at his back, imprisoned with him, biting him: Dante's portrait of implacable rage and hatred passed beyond death, yet now it seemed the players in this appalling drama had shifted and it was me, buried to the shoulders with this apparition behind me.

I took a faltering step into the kitchen, the door swinging wide before me, and tried to speak. What came out was a dry whisper, a broken plea:

"What do you want?"

The thing sitting on my kitchen chair jerked, as if startled, then slowly raised its head to look at me. I found that standing before the thing, watching this movement, was an act of courage in itself. I shuddered; the flesh on my arms humped into waves of gooseflesh large enough for me to see. I felt the contraction of subcutaneous muscles and it seemed that my flesh itself was attempting to move away from this affront to the world of warmth and daylight. Jardine's face was awful, a pallid smudge punctured by bruised eye sockets, the only pale thing in the room. He said nothing, but the scant light glittered on the surface of his eyes, giving a sense of an unpleasant intelligence.

Then there was a shift in the balance of shadows, a subtle resignation of presence, and the kitchen chair was empty. I took a convulsive breath, as if waking, or breaking the surface of deep water. Tiny bits of moonlight, bounced by the snow, came in under the kitchen blind and lay where Jardine had been. Emboldened by a blessed relief I took a step forwards and placed the palm of my hand on the chair: nothing. It was cold and apparently untroubled. I knelt and looked at the floor by the chair legs: again nothing, no large and spreading pool of blood. I stood, too quickly, and once again felt faint. The sound of my own pulse in my ears magnified and became a tidal crash. Silver edged flowers bloomed in my vision and died away to violet after-echoes. I swayed and put out a hand.

In the centre of the kitchen table was a pile of paperwork: bills and suchlike that I had been meaning to sort for the shredder, and I clutched at this tiny domestic detail, this sliver of normality, like a drowning man clutching a life-preserver. I stared at them, gradually recovering.

When the light went on I cried out and wheeled towards the door, instinctively raising my hands. My expression must have been startling because Ruth stopped rubbing sleep-puffed eyes and took a wary step backwards. I met her in the doorway, obeying an urge not to have her come into the room where he had been.

"Jesus, Jack, you scared me."

My heart was still thumping in my chest, my skin still cold but slick with sweat. What did she know about fear?

"Were you sleepwalking?"

And a second flood or relief washed through me. Yes, God yes. The almost overwhelming sense of dread – as if the feeling lived in every part of me and had moved out somehow through my skin, a shadow, a dark miasma inhabiting the house. The staginess of it: the walk down the stairs and Jardine sitting there, slyly waiting; it all had a dreamlike quality. My relief was so great that I hugged her, standing there in the doorway, loving the real and familiar feel of the fabric of her t-shirt, her bed-warmth. For a moment she stiffened in surprise, then hugged me back: simple animal comfort.

In the morning I woke with the dawn light creeping in through the curtains, a light so faint at first that only the gradual definition of the edges of the dresser, or the outline of the window sill made it apparent. I lay still, letting my mind run again through the cycle of tension and relief, then gently swung my legs out of bed to make for the bathroom.

I froze, looking down at the carpet where I had almost put my feet. Dried maroon in the half light, robbed of its lustre by time, penny-sized drops of blood lay almost in a figure eight pattern.

I saw it clearly: Jardine's left arm, hidden almost to the fingertips by his ragged sleeve, swinging slightly from the shoulder as he stood, inches from the bed, and watched us sleeping. I put my hand across my mouth to stifle a cry. I counted the drops and there were at least twelve: he had stood there for four or five minutes. Right there. That appalling face, dead eyes regarding us, curled and defenceless in sleep, the mind behind it incomprehensibly sly and dark, considering us. I closed my eyes for a moment, wishing it away, but when I opened them the pattern was still there. I reached downwards with trembling fingers and felt the stiff peaks in the carpet; the blood was powdery on my fingertips and had a coppery smell. I sat down heavily on the bed, holding my fingers far away from me. Ruth woke.

"Do you see this?"

She shrank away from me slightly, trying to blink away the light, and then came forwards.

"What is it?"

"Blood. I really think that it's blood."

Seven

I began the same spiral as Jardine, slower than him, as I had more in the world to keep me anchored and steady: a partner, parents; but I felt myself on the same downward curve.

I found sleep almost impossible and when I did knock myself out with alcohol or sleeping pills I would wake every forty minutes or so, unwilling to open my eyes in case he was standing close to me. During the day, when I closed my eyes an image of the gargoyles would rise, unbidden and unwelcome, their expression of rage and pity sloughing and melting and becoming Jardine's face: the glitter of malice in his eyes. All the time I strained to hear that steady drip that was his herald. I thought I heard it underscoring the traffic noise as I lay stiff and still in bed; in concert with the clanking ancient radiators as I waited for my students in the shared teaching room at the college; standing in a brightly lit aisle at the supermarket; it was everywhere. I began to come late and ill-prepared to classes. Ruth treated me at first with baffled compassion, then some resentment. I do not know how, at that point, she explained the blood on our carpet to herself, but I would offer her no explanation, and when I returned from college that day she had cleaned it up, leaving nothing but a soapy fresh smell.

Sometimes I travelled to college with a kitchen knife in my laptop case, at the top, where I could get to it quickly and easily and another, smaller paring knife in my coat pocket. Sometimes I would take one or the other out and watch how their keen edge split the light. I wondered what I meant to do with them, they could not, surely, be used to harm a dead man.

The temperature hovered around freezing, often diving well below that between two and four in the morning, a time when I was often coldly awake and listening. I began to check the weather app on my phone with absurd regularity – four or five times an hour, hoping, sometimes praying for a change. The blue cast of the graphics and the symbols used for below zero temperatures, ice and snow took on a mocking cast, and I watched the sunrise and sunset times, a record of the shortening winter days, with morbid fascination.

Though Jardine did not appear again I knew that he was circling me, gaining some momentum; I was a haunted man. The creaking floorboards and half-glimpsed figures, the feeling of chill, or of being watched that literature had led me to expect are a gross simplification. I experienced all of those things, but I knew that they were metaphors for a deeper malaise, a global thing, a complete attitudinal shift, like the symptoms of a mental illness - paranoia or a manic phase; he was everywhere. I saw footprints in the mud or the snow by the front door, malformed prints that suggested to the mind a lingering presence, and knew he had been there. I saw a figure in the landscape, glimpsed in the distance but drawing inexorably closer, a figure out so far on the periphery of vision that he *was* the landscape, out in the snow between the trees, or at the end of the street as evening came on. He was a figure looking at me with vapid interest from the edge of an old photograph, and his sobs, the dripping of his blood, were in the heartbeat of all of the music I heard.

Eight

When Christmas finally arrived we accepted an invitation to spend it with my parents. Driving there with a car full of gifts, heading for that strange lull between Christmas and New Year in my childhood home, I felt a little better. As the car passed through the Stokenchurch cutting, steep sides of chalk rising almost fifty metres on either side of the motorway, I felt that I might be leaving something behind, as if the cutting were a gateway through which Jardine might not pass. As we came out of it Ruth pointed out a red kite, rising over the winter fields, hunting over the dusting of snow, and I took it to be a good omen.

When we arrived it became obvious to me just how worried Ruth had been. Clearly she had discussed something of my recent shift in personality with my parents. My mother's hug was a little longer than I would have expected. My father put his hand on my shoulder and held my gaze as he asked me dad-stuff: were the roads free of snow and idiot drivers? Was it too early for a drink? Everyone was a little too careful in their choice of conversation, as if the wrong topic might cause me some fatal breakdown, but eventually seasonal busyness wore away the brittle frost. Ruth and my mother headed out in search of last-minute Christmas necessities – my sister and Owen, Evie and Julia were staying for Christmas and Boxing day. My father and I were charged with completing the decoration of the house, and this fossil of childhood was a comfort.

False jollity is better than none at all it turns out, and Christmas day passed in a blur of alcohol and glitter and tinsel. At lunch we wore ridiculous paper hats and ate far too much. Again I was aware of a brittleness to proceedings. Ruth was too quiet, everyone else too loud. My sister's children were shrill and excited. I felt all of them waiting for some signal from me that things were okay, but I could not think of what it might be, there was no way of cancelling out my haggard look and my watchful silence. As they passed food and conversation around me I tried to join in. I laughed at the Christmas cracker jokes and perhaps something started to loosen.

After lunch, whilst others took care of the washing up, I played a ridiculous game with my youngest nephew. He was five, and the thing consisted of a barrel into which players inserted plastic cutlasses until at one random sword-poke a rascally pirate popped out of the barrel, making everyone jump. Oblivious to the weird atmosphere over lunch, he giggled like a loon each time the stupid thing popped up. It was infectious, I found myself giggling along, crying a little with the intensity of it. As he reloaded for another try he looked up at me seriously: small brown hands and small brown eyes.

"Are you alright uncle Jack?"

We were in the corner of the large room, sitting on the carpet amongst the pine needles that the tree had dropped and small bits of screwed up wrapping paper. Over on the sofas conversation continued; nothing changed, but I felt attention settle upon us.

"I'm okay Owen." And it sounded right enough, firm enough to the room's adults, it seemed, as I pushed another cutlass into the barrel. The sense of attention shifted. Owen was not so easily fooled and looked out of the window at the dusting of snow on my parents' lawn, his small brow creased into a furrow.

"Mummy said that you might be sad."

"I was. But I feel better now."

And it was a little true. It was harder to imagine something as awful as Jardine in this room with its paper chains and Christmas tree. Soon we were playing the pirate game in teams, organised by the children. After that more games, drunken charades, balloon tennis. On Christmas night I slept almost untroubled in the spare room that used to be my father's office when I was a child, curled up with Ruth on a sagging bed; it was my first proper rest in weeks.

Nine

The Boxing Day Walk was a tradition that stretched back to a date long before my birth, started during my father's early childhood immediately following the war. There was a puritan element to it, as if two days of over-indulgence had to be balanced somehow, new toys forsaken for a few hours, the TV left behind. The weather was usually mild, but not this year. Boxing day dawned clear and very cold. There had been further snowfall in the night, and looking out onto the field that backed my parents' house I could see frost winking in the trees and glinting like diamonds on its surface. I knew that if you bent and raked that snow away and touched the black soil underneath it would be as hard and unforgiving as iron, and as the day grew older the sky would lose its high powder blue and become a louring white that would give snow again. My phone confirmed my suspicions: sunrise at eight-o-six, sunset at three fifty seven, high of two, low of minus six, clear morning skies, clouding with a promise of snow by noon.

Cold's part of it ... it gets in you.

I felt a prickle of fear, and heard movement behind me but it was Ruth, stirring in the old guest bed, the hardly-used linen crackling around her body.

Washing up our lunch things, with a lace of soap on her hands, my mother asked me to go find my dad.

"He always ducks out of this bit, and it's his job really, the quicker it's done the quicker we get out there."

I found him in the upstairs hallway, looking up through the open loft hatch with one hand pressed to the small of his back.

"What's up?"

He looked around, distracted, perhaps a little tipsy from lunch.

"Thought I could hear dripping in the loft again. Hot water tank, something like that, but I'm buggered if I can find it."

When he saw my expression he sobered quickly and actually took a step backwards, away from me, before coming in closer.

"What *is* it Jacky? Do you really think you killed that boy?"

He waited only a beat, not long enough for me to answer.

"He would have found something else to set him off. If you hadn't been there, you know. He would have chosen someone else to use as an excuse. He was ill, do you understand? Like a rusty nail sticking out of a fence. He was waiting to snag someone, and it turned out to be you."

I thought that this was apt, that my father was right, but not in the way he thought. There was an undercurrent of irritation in his voice, as if in my position he would have already worked this out and moved on. I saw Jardine sitting in the kitchen, the implacable hatred in his gaze, heard his rasping voice *... il traditor che io rodo ...*

No. He wasn't going to let me move on.

"Buck up, Jacky. I won't have this thing ruin Christmas for you - for all of us."

I blinked at the domestic simplicity of this; wishing fervently for such mundane concerns. What had Noble said about the Chilean girl, that she had shown him the contempt of one who is drowning, and sees another on the shore calmly discussing the weather. At that moment I hated him a little. I glanced up at the yawning loft hatch.

"Do you think we end when we die, dad?"

The question startled him, and he laughed. It was an old bone to pick, this one. Started on when I was five or so and answered with carefully neutral statements. Argued over in my teens, where I found my dad's simple and rational 'no-one knows, but I suspect we just end' unsatisfactory.

When he saw that I was serious, he became serious also, and gave it thought and careful phrasing, the way he had when I was five.

"Well, I doubt that there's a Heaven or Hell, if that's what you mean. But no-one really know what makes consciousness, do they? Is it electrical signals in the brain? An illusion created by instinct and memory? Is it a function of the soul? If we don't know precisely how consciousness is created, how can we say how and when it ends? Maybe we do go on somehow. I must say, as I get older the idea has more appeal."

He patted my shoulder as if this might be a comfort. Below us I could hear the kids scrabbling in the hall cupboard for their boots. It took courage, but I reached up past him and closed the loft hatch over our heads, then slid the latch over with my thumb. My mind conjured an image of Jardine, slumped on the rafters against the far wall, sitting in between the boxes that contained the books I couldn't be bothered to move, old stereo equipment and my parents' suitcases. As the hatch closed, the reflected light moved from the dark shining surface of his eyes like two sunsets and he waited in the dark, smiling faintly, as some plan for me formed in his dead mind.

I shuddered and followed my dad down to the kitchen

Around me my family became banners flying in the monochrome countryside. Brightly coloured coats, scarves and hats, the children shouting and running, making streamers of sound, Greg – my mother's white terrier - yipping and making sudden runs around our feet. I watched my father lock the front door then turn and open his jacket so I could see the glint of the hip flask there. He dropped me a large theatrical wink. Ruth saw it and smiled, her cheeks already reddening in the cold. A frown creased her forehead when I could not return her smile. I looked at my phone and it confirmed what the exposed skin of my face and hands was telling me: minus three, falling as evening came on.

There was a route, quickly established when my parents moved into the house years before, and now impossible to deviate from. Gather in the garden, then across the two-lane that led eventually into the village, walk along the edge of three fields, one with a proper hedgerow, two with weathered fences, then duck into the woodland proper between two hummocks whose capping trees had grown together and twisted into an embrace, making a gateway of sorts. It was more than two miles to the gateway, and by the time we reached it we were usually strung out into little groups.

I had retreated, become a coal burning deep inside the person that walked the woodland path, watchful and afraid. Owen lingered with us, picking up sticks and throwing them, kicking up snow as he ran, unable to understand my sudden quietness.

Behind the far end of the hedgerow there was sometimes a pony, dark brown, peering out from beneath a deep fringe. There was a ten inch gap in the twisted hawthorn foliage and the cold beast was standing and snorting just on the other side, a gatekeeper of the countryside, close enough for me to see the three of us drawn together in the convex surface of its eye. The thing shifted, snorting winter-breath again, then brought the other eye to the gap. Far away I could hear Evie and Julia shouting as they got away from us. Ruth had a small apple in the net siding of her backpack and she took it out and offered it with one slender hand.

"Come on, boy. Nice apple."

A soothing tone, welcoming and easy. She had spoken to me like that quite a lot in the last few weeks.

Owen crowded the gap. "He's got long lashes. How do you know it's a boy?"

She smiled faintly. "It's a mystical thing. Watch: a boy'll take the apple from me."

A few beats, then a snort of vapour breath, ancestor of the minotaur, as if the hedgerow were alive, a flash of square yellow teeth and the animal took the apple and crunched it noisily. Owen nodded.

"Do you think he's lonely in there?"

"Do you think animals get lonely?"

He squinted, his head on one side, trying to come to terms with this strange adult thought.

"Yep. Everyone gets lonely."

Ruth reached in through the hawthorn, trying unsuccessfully to pet the creature. Something in the failure of the gesture came in through the cold and touched me

"He's got us."

Another fey smile and a nod. Greg came back to us, panting and jumping so that he did not get snow on his belly. Owen broke away and followed him. I watched them running away up the lane. The snow had taken many of the simple markers for distance, and he seemed to chase the small dog along the side of the black hedgerow into a Breughel landscape, heading away over the snow into something with a skewed perspective, into something mediaeval.

Ruth rubbed the palms of her hands together. Over her shoulder I could see that, as predicted that morning, the sky had lost its pale blue and was bleached to a gravid white.

I heard a noise by the hedgerow and turned from her, seeking out its source.

"I really like you Jack. I really like all of this," She gestured at the lane stretching away, at my family's footprints in the snow. "But you've got to let go of this Jardine thing. The guilt. It's making you into someone different. I don't want you to be different. I want you to be happy and healthy."

I heard it again, slight and stealthy but unmistakeable this time, the slow drop of some liquid, falling and plashing against the surface of the snow. I became aware of how alone we were - the house a mile behind us, the village three miles away again. We were tiny dots of warm in a huge plane of winter and he could be anywhere. That sense of retreat increased. Ruth kept talking, kept *being*, but my attention shrank to a pencil beam sweeping backwards and forwards, trying to find the source of the sound. I fought to keep images of him from coming to my consciousness. He was standing behind the hedgerow, just out of our sight, one arm dangling, an uneven bloodied scarecrow; or he was waiting up ahead for us, sitting in a ditch as he had in his barn, legs open, blood spilling around him in a widening pool.

And then I saw it: snow melt. With its breath or body heat the pony had widened the bare patch of hawthorn and every once in a while a drip of melt-water was falling into a small pool near our feet. As afternoon became evening it would freeze into a slick little plate of ice. I glanced about me, feeling little relief, feeling that though it was stripped of ragged flesh and blood this was still a symbol, another marker of his presence in the day.

I began to back away from the hedgerow.

"We should catch everyone up."

Ruth shook her head, exasperated, but when she saw that I was serious, she followed.

I was in the Breughel landscape now, the pure white surface of the snow taking away perspective and making me feel lost in such a familiar place, as if reality were becoming more dreamlike, as if at any moment I might step into a ditch full of freezing water or have to walk half a day to reach our objective. The hawthorn hedge gave way to a ragged stake fence, almost six feet high and held together with panel nails and thick twists of rusting wire. I had not remembered how sharp the fence looked, like a grin of broken teeth. We reached the hummocks and the natural gate to the woodland and I paused there, one hand in my pocket, searching out the paring knife. Ruth had caught me up, and as we stepped through instinctively reached out and took my hand. She had taken off one woollen glove and her palm was small and warm. When I glanced at her, expecting her usual half-smile she gave instead a pained grimace.

"Are you okay?"

"No," she said, "I don't know what it is, but I feel... nervous." Then, a smile. "Could be Pan? You know?"

Incomprehension showed in my expression.

"The word 'panic' comes from the Greek god Pan. Some swain or maiden would be out in the countryside, like this, amongst the trees, and Pan would instil a terrible blind fear into them; a fear so big it seized them and threw them around, it would... who's there? Is someone there?"

The natural gateway gave in to an avenue of trees, sessile oak and beech with smaller scrubby trees in between. The avenue was perhaps a hundred metres long and then bent to the right. The woodland was managed to some degree, and it was one of forty or so avenues that eventually gave way to older, less formal arrangements of trees. Way up ahead I could hear Greg barking, but there were no voices. Ruth had taken a half step so that she was standing behind me, pointing down the avenue with one hand.

"I thought I saw someone there."

"Owen?"

"No. No. A man in a black coat."

I followed her pointing finger but found that the light was bad, getting worse as the sun came down in an arc behind the pall of clouds, and the trees gave good cover. There - that could be shoulders and a pale smudge of face far up, almost at the avenue's end - then it seemed to merge into the bole of the tree and its pattern of twisting branches. Instinctively I took a step away, wanting to be away from this place, but then my mind over-rode my body. Place didn't matter; Jardine could be anywhere.

"Still see him?"

She looked carefully, stretching slightly onto tiptoe.

"I don't think so. He was watching us."

"Owen? Owen, are you near?"

No answer. Half way down the avenue of trees a bird quit its perch and launched itself skyward like a tiny whirring engine; snow fell from its branch and pattered on the weird pattern made by the snow lying on dead leaves below it, then there was cathedral silence, a familiar expectant silence. I could feel Ruth's nervousness, it was in her posture and the way she clutched at my hand, her hard breathing. The fact that she could feel it too, a coalescing sense of danger coming from the woodland before us made it yet more real to me. I looked both ways along the lane as if for help, but none was forthcoming, there was nothing but stillness and chilly air, dark trees and white snow. My family were in those woods somewhere up ahead. If he had not caught up with my sister, then Owen was rambling between those trees with only Greg for company.

"Jardine?"

I had called his name before my mind could intervene. I felt Ruth's hand slacken in mine and then grip it again with renewed force. The fact that she did not draw away to question me, to tell me that I was insane to be calling a dead man's name out into the blank rows of trees had a terrible finality. Either she had become infected by my terror, or she thought that she had identified her apparition in the trees, and now she had seen him too.

Amongst the trees the light lost all of its potency, it was the ghost of light, an echo only, hanging in the air ready to be swept away by the night.

"Owen? Anyone?"

Silence again, no animal sounds. It was colder here too and a few snowflakes fell with my flat and echoless shout. We moved onto the ragged path, still clutching each other. It was hard to walk on. There were several sets of prints on the snow, some small, some large. Around them the snow masked the path's uneven surface and patches of ice and we stumbled and moved slowly. As we neared the point where I thought the figure had been I saw one set of prints veer off from the others at an angle. These were odd prints, one foot always more definite than the other, as if the person who made them had worn only one shoe. Their presence seemed to relieve Ruth and she panted out an almost hysterical giggle.

"Look: prints. Someone walking a dog or something, that's all."

I could not take my eyes from them.

"I want to follow them for a little while."

"Why?" She gestured out along the pathway. "We should find everyone else."

"I just … need to *see*."

I didn't finish the sentence '*where he is*'. It was the logic of the nerves and not of the mind. If I could see him, then there was a chance I could keep some distance between us. Not waiting for argument I started off after the prints, leaving the path, trying to move stealthily but forced to use comic, ungainly strides to get across the snow where it had settled into drifts almost a foot deep. Ruth followed, unwilling to be left alone.

For a while I could hear nothing but our breathing and the creak and crunch of snow compacting under our feet. The prints kept to a path diagonal to that which my family would have taken, skirting between the trees, but moving through the undergrowth, so that I had to push through thorn bushes and at one point climb over a small dead-fall. As I turned to take Ruth's hand to help her over I heard quiet laughter. It was low, rasping and sinister. There was nothing that could normally be described as humour in the sound, it was sunless and hungry and cruel. As I looked around for a hunched figure in the trees I caught sight of Ruth's face: pale and frightened, eyes and mouth wide. I could see no-one else, and then the sound came again. I could not locate it. It seemed to come from everywhere at once, as if it might be emanating from deep under the earth.

"Where is he?"

A desperate whisper. Again I looked around but could see nothing. The snow was falling in earnest now, coming down in unfathomable patterns created by the tree limbs twisting above us – some places were free of it, in others the snow fell in mini-storms, twisting around unseen currents of air.

"Uncle Jack?"

Where? Where did it come from? A small voice, thin and reedy, almost paralysed by fear.

Was it Owen, or a mocking impersonation? When I replayed the voice in my head I could not tell, and again it seemed impossible to localise. I waded in one direction, faintly aware that Ruth had not followed, and bent into the snow, one hand held up above my eyes, turning, trying to see, but I saw nothing but an expanse of black and white.

Then, a sound that I could locate, piercingly loud: a high-pitched animal keening. It was so awful, filled with such pain and panic that for a moment the scene before me stopped making any sense. Black hulks of trees and white drifts and swirls of snow fractured and became incomprehensible shapes reaching towards me. I was on the point of panic, of allowing some deeper animal part of my brain to take over and rush me off through the trees, probably screaming and crying myself. I sank to one knee and I had to reach forwards and grasp the trunk of a tree before me. The sound kept on and on, rising slightly in pitch, dissolving into whimpers before rising again.

Yes. It was definitely east of me, away from the weakening sunlight. Now I did run, not away, but towards the sound, getting into an avenue of trees and following that scream to its source, blundering through the snow, panting and almost crying with the effort, powder billowing around me. It stopped suddenly, leaving after-echoes in my mind and I saw it too late, much too late: a hunched shadow slicked to the side of a tree that seemed to detach itself as I passed. By the time I had processed this image I knew that he had already stepped out and was standing behind me. The certainty came into my mind, stealthy as the falling snow, that he was regarding me with his dead eyes and that his blood was falling onto the snow, and I was too afraid to turn around and face him, to *see*, and then I had the impression that one of the trees nearby, a great oak, had been uprooted and had fallen onto me, crushing me beneath it.

I awoke and it was later. More of the colour was gone from the day and it was colder. The side of my face hurt and my hand came up to feel it and I picked sharp black bits of bark out of my skin, amazed to see my own blood on my fingers. The snow had gotten into my clothing somehow and chilled me. The back of my hand had a bluish sheen and I found my wrist and fingers difficult to bend.

Snow had fallen into my face and I had to blink its shapes out of my eyelashes.

I could hear dripping, not far off, behind me and just feet away: slow, measured, and it caused me to curl up, to bring my knees up to my chest and my arms over my face and sob like a child; whatever there was for me to see there, I did not want to see it. There are worse things than seeing, however, and I began to imagine him approaching, the lonely creak and crunch of compacting snow as he walked towards me, the shift in the light and in my awareness as his bloodied face, teeth bared, came closer to mine.

My eyes sprang open wide as I rolled over and I was blinded by the scene before me. Pure white, the snow seeming to radiate light that it had kept from earlier in the day, cut in half by a thick black line, the purity of this symmetry spoiled by several rounded shapes. Details came in. The thick line was the bole of a tree. Hunched in its shadow was a small figure.   A tiny face, too pale, hanging downwards towards the snow, legs parted, one arm outflung in a familiar pose, around him a widening pool of blood.

"Ow-en."

I panted out the word, struggling to my knees. The blow I had taken to the side of my head had done something to ruin my balance and I took two steps away from where I wanted to be and flopped over into the snow again, on my side, it rose around me in a powdery spray. He was Jardine in miniature, the replication of the pose exact. I lay panting in the snow, collecting my energy. Far off I heard a shout, unmistakeably my father, all of them returning down the path. They must not see him like this.

I dragged myself to my knees, swaying with the effort, and crawled towards him, feeling the stones and twigs digging into my knees as they sank through the layer of snow. When I reached him I put out my hands to touch him and for a moment drew back. He would be cold. He must be dead; there was so much blood around him, obscene in the whiteness. Then he moaned, a thick sound, deep in his throat and that broke my paralysis. Bleeding could be stopped. I took his hand in mine (knowing it would be the left, he would have cut the left) and raised it over the level of his heart, pulling back the sleeve of his coat. His arm was completely coated, slick and horrible under my fingers. I wiped my hand in the snow, leaving an awful red smear, and then wiped his wrist, unable to see a wound. I took a handful of snow and rubbed his arm, almost to the elbow: nothing but pale flesh under the red smears. His face still hung downwards and I reached forwards and lifted it, holding his chin. His head came up, but it was heavy.

Something dripped into the snow next to me. I saw it as if in slow motion: a large viscous drop, carrying an awful sheen. It landed in the whiteness, burying itself beneath the surface, then spread out, giving the snow around it a pink tinge.

I looked upwards, my head full of visions of Jardine suspended in the air above me somehow, ready to descend, but all I could see was Greg, impaled upon a branch perhaps eight feet above my head. The branch entered his body just behind the hind hips and came out below his ribcage. He hung from it, completely lifeless. Blood had run from the wound and was still dripping from his white fur, from the end of his snout and even from his distended tongue, a steady and familiar drip that had infected my world like the worst plague and was now landing on Owen, propped unconscious against the tree.

Another call. My name? Owen's? Sharp concern in the voice, but no fear. I could feel my pulse thudding in my chest and moments later repeating in the side of my head. With each beat it seemed a wall of darkness, an absurd blankness, like an impenetrable fog inched into my vision from the left. With a convulsive heave I moved Owen around the tree base and out from under poor Greg. His head lolled and his eyes fluttered open briefly, but thankfully there was no recognition there. I bent to hug him, hoping to share some warmth and looked out along the avenues of trees.

We were at a crossroads of sorts, at the centre of this part of the woodland, and if I closed my left eye I could still see a few hundred yards each way through the falling snow. A flash of colour to the west: my sister's jacket, bobbing as she ran. I tried to call and she came on faster. Breathing hard I glanced around again. The movement sent a wave of pain racing down from the side of my head into my left arm, and the wall of dimness began to inch across my vision again. Aware now that I was breathing hard, panting, and I was slicked with sweat, I rested my head on the tree.

Behind me, to the east, in the corner of what I could see and fading into the snow there was a darker figure, a hateful uneven silhouette half eclipsed by a tree. I took one hand from Owen and tried to reach the knife in my pocket. It was him. One shoulder was higher than the other, one arm dragging almost into the snow. A pale smudge of face punctured by bruised and reddened eyes that regarded me with vapid hunger. I tried to turn my head, to see him more clearly, to see if he was moving towards me, but the movement caused him to be caught by the wall of dimness eclipsing my vision and he faded into the fog. When only his draggling left arm was visible I felt a wave of nausea flood through me, and then I lost consciousness.

Ten

In a dimly lit room I lay looking at a battered chair. There were chips and small gouges in the wooden arms, and it was grubby. For long spaces of time I regarded these patterns of wear and tried to read them with foolish cunning. They were a map of the world, spread and twisted; they were felled trees, intertwined, their branches could not be followed to any conclusion; they were pools of blood, spreading out and reaching for one another. I felt pain in the side of my head: of course, it was full of sharp bits of bark. As I moved, they moved, digging in there.

A parade of phantoms occupied the chair. They tried to tell me things, but I could not hear them. A policeman in a crisp uniform, leaning forwards and talking, then stuttering back to sit in the chair with his arms folded, regarding me sternly. His hat was on his head, then off on his knees then on the floor by the chair side, then on again. In childish joy I tried to ask him how this trick was done, but remained mute.

He became Ruth, still wearing her winter jacket and boots and jeans with mud on the knees. A faded Ruth, drained of most of her colour, subject to some photo-effect that bleached her of vitality. She cried steadily, even as she took off her jacket. I saw her holding a hand and knew that it must be mine, but I felt nothing. She spoke, regretfully, earnestly but none of it came in to me.

For a brief time Noble was there, live Noble, storytelling Noble in a grey suit. He reached out a sorrowful and consoling hand and became my father, angry and gesturing, reproachful and sleepless. He strutted and blustered to no avail and in disgust became Detective Hopper, neat and self contained, regarding me keenly with open curiosity. Hopper did not speak or plead or gesture, but only waited in the dim room, one knee crossed over the other.

Hopper was there, unmoving, for aeons. I noticed that now he was wearing a tan raincoat. He had been caught in a shower, perhaps. Perhaps a light fall of rain had wet his shoulders as he came to this room and the efficient material of his wondrous coat had beaded the rain and now it ran in harmless rivulets from his shoulder, down his long left arm, where an occasional drip of water fell to stain the floor.

Dreamlike fear, like the dull tone of a bell stretching out and colouring everything. Water to blood; not a tan raincoat but a black jacket, almost hiding long pale fingers. If I looked upwards I would see not Hopper's disconcertingly intelligent gaze, but a strange dead galaxy in Jardine's reddened pupils.

I screamed and thrashed and tried to crawl away and sudden light infiltrated the room and changed everything and it was none of these people trying to calm me and keep me to the bed. Instead it was a nurse in pale blue scrubs, concerned and wary and pushing a bell to summon others. Lights came on, banishing the shadows and I felt better.

More nurses and a doctor. She shone a light in my eyes and watched, arms folded, as one of the nurses asked me obvious questions and tested my reflexes. There was a large dressing on the side of my head that throbbed dully, she investigated it with gentle fingers, frowning, then read some notes from a clipboard.

"You were very lucky Dr. Garrod."

I blinked uncomprehendingly. I was not lucky.

"You sustained quite an injury there." A flick of one fingertip towards my head. "There was a small bleed inside your skull but it has subsided, I would guess before it could cause you any lasting damage."

I tried to sit up and she stepped forwards quickly and put a hand on my chest.

"You need to rest, Dr. Garrod. If you cannot do that on your own I will sedate you."

A CAT scan, another consultant, and a period of pharmaceutically-aided rest. When I awoke I became aware of a shadow in the open doorway of my room, and voices entering from outside. I saw that Hopper was standing in the doorway, wearing his raincoat and watching with his unswerving gaze. My doctor stood next to him, again looking at some notes and frowning.

"Ten minutes," she said. "No more. Do not agitate him."

Hopper made no promises, but watched mildly as she hung the notes on my bed and left.

He sat down in the chair, crossed his legs and looked at me.

"Did it rain?"

"I'm sorry?"

"When you were here before. Did it rain?"

He shook his head.

"No. It's been foggy and damp. You said some strange things whilst I was here."

I was too tired, too beaten to feel any wariness or shame.

"I did?"

"You did. You apologised for killing Jardine, for one. Not to me, but to him."

The bitter irony of this was not lost on me, I giggled foolishly, dimly aware that I was still a little stoned.

"I didn't kill Jardine."

"So it seems. In fact you were also certain that he was still alive. You spoke to him at length and told a constable, then me, then anyone else who would listen that Jardine attacked you in the woods."

The truth was simpler than any fabrication.

"He did."

As if from far away, from a vantage point I could never physically have reached, I saw the snowy scene: the tree, Greg, Owen slumped beneath him in a pool of blood, and tried to sit up again.

"Is Owen?"

Hopper put out a hand to quell me.

"They're all fine; except for your parents' dog. Your nephew was released from hospital after a day's observation; he has scratches on his arm and remembers very little. A paramedic found Miss Moore wandering in the woods about half a mile from you – confused about what happened, but none the worse for wear. She has made a statement and returned to Oxford. She calls here every two or three hours."

The dope was good stuff, my responses were dulled. I felt only a mild relief infusing this grey exhaustion. He leaned forwards, placing one forearm on his knee, not taking his gaze from me.

"I saw him buried, you know. Autopsy photographs, DNA identification. Impossible to fake."

I shrugged, a painful movement for me, and only one shoulder came up. He drew a phone from his pocket and held it out, showing me the controls for a Dictaphone app, then dropped it onto the coverlet of the bed.

"I need you to tell me what you think happened, as succinctly as you can. Don't lie. This won't form part of any formal statement. Strictly speaking this isn't my case; but it would be helpful."

I did so, not bothering to replace Jardine's name with that of another, or cover him over with 'I thought I saws', such politeness seemed ridiculous.

When I had finished Hopper sat back, slipping the phone back into his pocket. The dim hospital-room lamp put tiny reflected lights in his eyes. His face showed puzzlement and some faint concern, as if I had passed on a particularly difficult crossword clue to him. When he spoke I detected neither scorn nor a sense that he was humouring a sick man.

"Do you know what's spooky? I think you believe it."

I gave no response. He took a photograph from inside his folder and laid it on the bed, facing me. I flinched away from it.

It showed Jardine's body, a still taken from the film he had shot.

"Your sister was first on the scene - after you - and she described it very clearly. I don't believe it is a scene she will ever forget. Your name brought the report to my computer, and the similarity between this," he tapped the photo, "and what happened to your nephew struck me immediately."

"When they found out about you, Dorset CID wanted to run with the idea that you did it. That for whatever reason you've gone completely batshit, did this thing to your own nephew – set it up to look like Jardine's death - and then you ran into a big tree branch whilst trying to get away."

"That's not what happened."

He nodded. "True. I talked them down. It doesn't fit the forensic evidence at the scene very well, or the pattern of your injury. Also, though your family think you've been behaving oddly recently, none of them – not even your sister – seem to think you could do this. Also your account and Miss Moore's account tally pretty well until you split up, and I made sure that you haven't talked to each other. How well did you know Jardine?"

The question was low-pitched, part of the sentence, apparently casual, designed to throw me off balance in some way I did not yet understand.

"Not well at all. He was just a rival at work. Academics aren't particularly collaborative."

"Why did he say you worked together in his video?"

"I don't know. He was about to die. He said all sorts of things."

"Right. He was... an interesting man, Dr. Jardine. Did you know he was wealthy?"

"No."

"Yes; a millionaire several times over. He owned that house at Wytham great wood, and others. Properties in Oxford and London. His family are all dead, all apart from some maiden aunt in Scotland, did you know that?"

"No."

"I think someone that powerful and... eccentric could be very difficult."

I began to laugh, a weak horrible laughter that turned into a coughing fit, he regarded me mildly.

"I think Jardine killed himself and for reasons I cannot begin to fathom, hired someone to frighten you. Do you think that's possible?"

No. It was Jardine. "Anything's possible."

"I suppose so." Oddly, he sounded as if he believed this.

"Do you think you pissed him off that badly?"

"Yes."

I looked towards the window where hospital blinds shut out the early evening darkness. Where was he now? Did he exist when I could not see him? Was he shuffling along the dark road towards the hospital, or towards my house? Was he waiting, silent and cold, in the shadows made by the streetlight that crowned our driveway, or did he wait away in some eternal limbo, the ultimate vantage point from which to view and then re-enter my life at just the right point. Instinct and jangled nerves told me that all of these were true. He was everywhere and nowhere, waiting in the cold, waiting *for* the cold.

I blinked, the sedative in my system both helping and slowing my thinking. I realised that there had been some shift in the situation, a change of timbre in some long and repeating chord that had accompanied my life for weeks, a feeling of imminence quashed, of present danger abated.

"Has the weather changed?"

Hopper showed faint surprise, there and then gone very quickly. I realised how carefully he had managed our exchanges, how all of his apparent spontaneity was a sham. He must be a very good policeman.

"It has. Typical Christmas now – warm and wet. The snow's mostly gone, It's probably eleven or twelve degrees out there."

I swung my legs from the bed, hobbled to the window, and struggled with the unfamiliar controls of the blinds. He watched me impassively for a moment then rose and reached over my shoulder to pull the strings.

The blind rose to reveal a white bank of mist. We were on the third floor and craning my neck I could just see the edge of the car park: a few feet of concrete, the fronts and backs of Fords and Nissans and Volvos. I breathed on the glass, hard, and my condensed breath disappeared almost immediately.

"Where's my phone?"

He looked in the nightstand and found it there. I turned it on and waited. The old compulsion guided my fingers. I allowed data and stroked the weather app. Sunrise: eight-oh-six, sunset: three-fifty-eight, ten degrees tonight, twelve tomorrow. I scrolled through the week – according to the Met office the temperature would not drop below freezing until almost the New Year.

I reeled away from the foggy window, almost dancing in a kind of drugged exultation, knowing that somehow a warm snap would mean he could not come. I went back to the window and looked again, close to the glass. Somehow he was bound up with the cold, and he could not come.

My joy was short lived, and Hopper saw my expression change from exultation to fear as I seemed to hear a hiss of frustration and see the spit shining on his bared teeth as in rage Jardine screamed and angled in towards the window, close to my face, but was denied by the fog. It was as if a savage dog were growling and snarling, held on a leash inches before my eyes. I backed away from the window, collapsing onto my hospital bed, and the feeling fell away like an echo. Hopper was at my side quickly, looking over his shoulder at the blank glass as if he too had sensed something there. I breathed deeply, trying to clear my head, dimly aware of a nurse appearing in the doorway.

"How long?" I muttered. How long could the warmth last?

Eleven

I became a child again, losing my adult sense of time. It stretched and warped. I would check the window and see damp concrete and fog, doze for a few seconds and dream of ice forming on the hospital gutters and rain freezing into treacherous patterns by the hospital doors, then rise a few minutes later and check again. I begged my doctor to release me from the hospital and after an eternity she relented and then there was another frustrating wait, sitting on the edge of three different beds as I was shuffled from ward to ward so that different departments could okay my discharge and dispense pills and hurried advice.

My father picked me up, huddled into his overcoat in a way that suggested that he didn't want to touch me. He kept things quiet and low key, driving with excessive care. A mile from his home he pulled the car into a lay-by and we sat, listening to traffic pass us and disappear into the fog five metres or so ahead.

"Are you okay?"

I found that I did not know how to answer such a simple and direct question.

"Not really."

"How does your head feel?"

"It hurts."

"The police have told us almost nothing. What did they tell you?"

"About the same. They're working on the idea that Jardine has hired someone to scare me."

My father looked ashen-faced. He had shaved badly, and there was a nick on the left side of his chin. Several cars passed by, tyres spattering stones and water.

"Your sister wants you to stay away from her and the children until this is over. The shock of finding you like that in the snow. She thought... "

He trailed off. What had she thought? That I had hurt Owen?

He saw the realisation dawning in my expression and went on.

"You have to understand, we were all hysterical. We didn't know if it was your blood, or Owen's, or Greg's. No-one could find Ruth. Until the police and the paramedics arrived it was awful. I've walked those woods for more years than I care to mention, and I... " He let out a ragged breath. "Fear is horrible, Jack. If that bastard wanted to frighten you then his purpose is served. He frightened all of us." He peered out into the fog ahead of the car, "I'm frightened now, like I haven't really come down, you know?"

I did. I wanted to feel communion with him, but he didn't *know* hadn't felt it fully. He wasn't afraid yet, not afraid the way I was. It was exhausting, as if I were perpetually running as hard and as fast as I could. Talking to my Dad was like having a terminal illness and trying to commiserate over someone's sunburn.

I spent an hour at my parents' house with my tearful mother. Greg's basket and bowl were gone from the kitchen, before my dad, with ill-disguised relief, drove me home.

I came home to a new Ruth, and I realised how it must have been for her for the last few months, to have someone you know well, someone you love, have something knocked out of them, making them emptier, greyer than they were. It was like mourning, as if some part of her were engaged elsewhere, dealing with an awful but undeniable fact. She opened the door slowly and looked at me with a mixture of relief and fear. By the door of the cupboard under the stairs there were two small suitcases and her backpack, they looked to be packed and ready to go. I ignored them. We shared odd bright small talk, as if we were acquaintances, while she made coffee and sat in the kitchen chair which Jardine had recently occupied. My mug was hot between my palms, the windows of the house were cataracted with fog, and moisture dripped from the guttering and the window sills, making me uneasy.

I quelled her chatter with simple questions.

"What happened to you? What did you see?"

A pinched, wounded expression, then she looked down towards the kitchen floor.

"I didn't see anything. I just got... lost. I saw you in front of me, running, then I got turned around and must have wandered away from you. I lost some time, then I heard someone calling out and a paramedic found me."

I knew her well enough to see the lie there. She had seen or heard something out in the snow, between those trees, but I also knew her well enough to see that she would not talk about it. I even knew how she felt; talking about it, telling it, would transform it from an internal to an external experience and give it more reality.

I nodded towards the suitcases in the hall.

"If I hadn't been discharged today, would you have left?"

A fat tear threaded its way slowly down the plane of her cheek then fell to the floor as she nodded.

"I was getting ready to. Jack, I just can't stand it, whatever it is. I'm scared and I don't really understand what's happening. I feel like I'm going insane and I just have this drive to get away from here."

"Where would you go?" A dull question; leave me then, leave me to drown.

"My parents have a holiday place in Florida; it was my grandparents' house. It's not... it's empty at the moment and it's not like here. It's warm all the time; warm and wet or warm and dry; no winter. I just want to be in the warm."

Then blessed words that came from her lips as the question dawned in my mind.

"Come with me. Please come, Jack. Even now it'll be warm there."

Hope is almost more terrible than fear. To be drowning and then suddenly in sight of the shore, struggling for it, produces greater desperation and fear.

Of course - somewhere that had no seasons, where there was no splendid decay of autumn and winter never ever came; perhaps we would be safe there. My phone lay on the table between us and I checked the weather app again. Over the next four days the temperature was due to fall, just a degree or so a day, until New Year, when a low pressure system over Iceland would shift, and a new cold front would arrive bringing with it a new freeze.

We could not have chosen a worse time to try to make emergency travel plans. The New Year rush was on, and the fog had caused some delays at British airports that meant a backlog of travellers. Finally, after hours on the internet and more time on the phone we managed to find two ways to get to Miami. One involved a stopover at Charles de Gaul, Paris, the other, eight hours later, was a first class cancellation. Together they would cost us over half of our savings, but neither of us raised an eyebrow. We decided that Ruth should fly first. I lied about my head injury so that I could fly. From the bedroom Ruth made a phone call to her parents. Her tone was slow and careful, explaining, asking; lord knows what they thought of this strange request from their wandering daughter. I left a message at Fletcher's office, knowing he would not be there to get it. For almost a day making arrangements kept us busy and exhausted, and we tied up our lives in Oxford as best we could.

Twelve

As a child I used to cook with my mother, baking, and we would always use the same large clear mixing bowl, something she had inherited from my grandmother. That night I dreamed of its simple domed shape, upturned and placed over my world like a thick glass prison, making the air itself heavy with compression, and the sounds we made dull and slow. During one of my days in the dome I looked upwards to see a form looming over it, a stooped and crooked form of such magnitude that it twisted me into cowering panic. High above I could see the glint of light in merciless eyes, the hunch of one arm held slightly forwards, blood dripping from the sleeve. A monstrous drop fell towards me; gallons of viscous blood spattered the dome and ran down it so that the whole world was patterned red.

Then there was the sound of a gentle rain tapping the windows. Lying next to me Ruth was muttering in her sleep: a grey form clutching the duvet, enclosed in her own horrible dream. 'No *no*. No *no...*' a constant litany of denial. I woke her by gently stroking her arm and she cried out and skittered away from me then relaxed. I made coffee and we waited for the morning.

The rain seeped down on us from a dull grey sky that barely seemed to lighten as the day came on. I could not escape the idea that this was some elaborate game of cat and mouse and that the rain that I saw running in rivulets down the taxi window, or pattering noiselessly on the plate glass of the passenger lounge at the airport was Jardine's reminder that I lay under his paw. Watching Ruth go was a cowardly agony. She was escaping before me. Checking in, boarding, then I watched her flight disappear into the grey sky and waited for my own.

I sat in a ridiculously luxurious seat looking out at grey London tarmac and counting to ten over and over, tapping my feet. I made the flight attendants nervous and they checked on me too often. Then take-off into that grey sky, piercing the clouds. London became a toy city, then unseen, then a memory.

I seemed to sleep, then awake into a dream that stretched on and on. Our plan went too well and we met at Miami International without a hitch. Ruth cried on my shirt, sobs of relief. I was numb. Through more plate glass I could see a high deep blue sky graced with a few tiny white clouds. I had moved from air-conditioned plane to air-conditioned airport, and it wasn't until we stepped outside, and I felt the warm Miami air, that some weight shifted inside me and I began to believe in our escape.

Again, my mind went to grief to try to describe our state. In the early days of grieving a loss sleep is a release, dreams are often brighter and more pleasant than waking life; there your mind escapes, for a while, the shadow that has fallen across you; there things are a different colour.

And it was blocks of simple colour that I noticed. The deep blue of the waters of the gulf as they met the sky in an unwavering line that seemed, to British eyes, to stretch on forever. The white line of highway impossibly close to the water. The city of Marathon like a cubist dream with its jetties and square low-slung architecture. It was about as far from Oxford as we could have come. Ruth grinned as she drove the rental car, a little Ford, and I found myself grinning back at her reflexively.

Her parents' place was a small wood-framed house on Yellow Creek Road in the city of Marathon, and everything about it pleased me – the artless simplicity of its single-story design which meant that the sunlight was everywhere and the water almost always in sight. Ceiling fans and tile floors and a huge terrace: it was a place built for the heat.

It was easier than I would have thought to leave our other lives behind. As long as the rent was paid on the Oxford house, all was well. Fletcher arranged a sabbatical for me, with some relief, I believe, and Ruth convinced her college that she was taking some time to write up, and to some extent this is what she did. My parents called the house, often at first, but then with decreasing urgency.

We did not talk about Oxford. We enjoyed the sea and the sky. In the evening we would watch the sunset, sometimes from the beach, sitting on a sun-bleached drift log we had adopted as our own, sometimes from the terrace. The sun would go down in red glory and the pelicans would rise across it in ungainly flight. Afterwards, like applause for some performance we would hear bait-fish leaping.

In those grief-dreams, though, there is a silent and regarding part of you which knows the truth. It watches from the background, as a parent watches the formless games of a child. It notes the symbolism of your dreams, symbolism that your playing self ignores: the sunset was often blood red, our sun-bleached log had salt patterns on its hide which brought to mind sloughing moon-white faces with puncture-wound eyes, I knew that I had conversations – with Ruth, with my parents – but I could not remember what was said. The sugar-coating of impermanence was on it all, so when it was brought to an end there was no surprise, just the faint tug of regret that none of it was real and I must return to a worse world.

The grey light of a morning I thought I had already lived, greeted me, and there was a steady knocking at the front door.

As in my dream, Ruth woke and skittered away from me, cowering away from the knocking sound. I rose and went to the door in my pyjamas. Our suitcases were still packed in the hallway. Through the glass of the door I could see someone waiting. I knew who it would be before the door came open.

"Detective Hopper."

Standing under an oversized umbrella he frowned at me, as if surprised to see me on my own doorstep. There was a patrol car parked by the gate with a couple of uniformed officers inside. Hopper looked past me and noticed the cases in the hall.

"Going somewhere Dr. Garrod?"

"Away from here. Miami. Ruth's parents have a place there." My image if it – paint peeling on the terrace rail, stray sand grains on the tiled kitchen floor came to me, then faded: ridiculous.

The policeman shook his head, he seemed genuinely grieved.

"No. Not today. Today you're coming with me."

Thirteen

And so we went, through the rain and the Oxford traffic. The squad car's windscreen wipers kept time, speeding up as we made it past the ring road and out of the city, heading north-west towards Wytham great wood and Jardine's farm house. I sat next to a stone-faced constable; Hopper sat up front, reading something on his phone.

We left the main road and drove slowly down a gravelled lane with a high yew hedge on one side, and a field on the other then turned through a wide wooden gateway into a scene of chaos. At first, all I could make out were the lights, two yellow and one orange each spinning out of sequence and at different heights, cutting through the grey in stripes to light up the rain splashes on the window in syncopated time. As our car came to a stop, a policeman rushed up to it, holding a sheaf of notes over his head to keep off the rain. Hopper got out, and I heard the other man say-

"One more, sir, and that's only a quarter of the total area. If he went out into the woodland, then

it's going to be harder. We'll need more dog units, probably methane kits."

Through the open car door I could see mud and rutted tracks filling with water on what had once been a wide lawn. After a moment Hopper came back, opened my door and beckoned me out. I followed him across the ruts, not bothering to step over the puddles. The lawn lay in the arms of a three-story farmhouse and two of its outbuildings, grey and utilitarian - unmistakeably barns. My attention was drawn by the one furthest from the house: that was where he had done it. The house had been extended twice on the ground floor, without regard for its aesthetics, and this gave it an uneven silhouette, as if it were hunched up on one side, a shoulder raised, jealously curling an arm around the lawn's edge. We moved to the threshold of its wide door, which afforded some shelter, and turned to look back. What was left of the lawn had been sectioned into squares, ten feet on an edge, by lengths of police tape strung around steel poles. The lights I had seen came from a truck and two earth movers. They still spun chaotically over the scene, and I tried to follow their beams through the grey rain but it was dizzying. Policemen in high-visibility clothing were everywhere, digging, sifting. One of the earth movers had its jaws in the soil, and as I watched, with a rev it dragged a rectangle of black soil out and upwards and dumped it to one side. Over everything fat raindrops fell in steady horizontal lines, plashing in the puddles and the mud, running in streams through the guttering of the house, drumming on Hopper's umbrella and the backs of the policemen working the lawn. With his mild eyes Hopper watched me take all of this in.

Another detective strode up to us, not bothering to shelter. He looked furious, ignored me and glared at Hopper.

"I've put in a call to headquarters north, Hopper. DCI Allen's on her way out here to stop this." Then he turned on his heel and strode away.

Hopper sighed and looked at me for a long moment, his head slightly on one side, as of trying to come to some decision. He muttered "at least twenty minutes to Kidlington. Okay." Under his breath, then, raising his umbrella higher-

"Come with me."

At the lawn's edge planks had been laid over the mud, and we had gone twenty feet before I realised our direction and stopped. Now ten feet ahead, Hopper turned.

"Come into the barn."

"I don't want to." I could feel the rain soaking through my hair and chilling my head. It was soaking through my coat in a crescent over my shoulder and wetting my back. It was in my eyes.

"Come into the barn."

I groaned, an involuntary sound and he actually held out his hand, as if he might be a parent encouraging a frightened child.

I followed him and the building loomed in front of me: a great low structure with wide double doors, horribly familiar. It had probably once been a threshing barn, but its wooden frame had been carelessly renovated with a tin roof and a cinderblock shell. I stepped inside and the noise of the rain on the roof was immense: a symphony of drumming, beyond rhythm; it sounded angry, as if it wanted us out of the barn and away. I looked for the wall against which Jardine had leaned as he died, but instead saw a trestle table holding documents and photographs. A uniformed officer stood over them, working. She glanced up when she saw us, Hopper nodded, and she left, disappearing into the curtain of rain. He stood at the table, sifting through, finding what he wanted and carefully laying it out, his shoulders moved, as if he were conducting an orchestra.

"We're on your land now, you know."

An uncomprehending silence.

"We found a copy of Jardine's last will and testament in the house. Another will be lodged with his solicitor, I'm sure. He left you the house for some reason."

A glance over his shoulder.

"You didn't know?"

A faint shake of my head.

"Come and look at these." He had to speak loudly to be heard over the rain, but this was unmistakeably an order. I found I did not want to look at the photographs.

Hopper turned fully. The images before him had sparked some terrible anger, and he could not keep it from his voice.

"Come and look."

As I moved towards him I was shaking my head and muttering 'no' under my breath. Still, I went, and looked at Hopper's grim haul of images.

He had arranged them well. They told an appalling story. There were three in the first row; similar, but not the same. Each showed a hole, dug in what I supposed to be the lawn outside. I saw bits of policemen in stop-motion: a boot, a trouser leg, a face half turned away in disgust. The holes were narrow, three feet square, but deep, sinking down six feet into the black clay. Digging them in the first instance must have been a peculiar labour of love. At the bottom of each was a round structure that at first I could not identify – then I saw a metal edge and suddenly the shape made sense: a barrel.

The next row showed two policemen running a block-and-tackle, powered by the winch on a Land Rover, hauling one of the barrels from the earth. One policeman was frozen, shouting something with an arm outstretched. Rain was falling on them in steady sheets, greying the air. The next image was inside somewhere, perhaps in the other barn, somewhere dry where they could set up proper lights. The top had been pried off of the barrel and was lying to one side, but the container's contents were obscured by angles. In the next image the police photographer had stepped forwards and pointed his lens directly into the barrel, sparing the viewer nothing. I saw a confusion of unidentifiable shapes, organic certainly, but a grey/green colour. Eventually my mind resolved these shapes into a tangle of limbs crowding around the crown of a head. I saw matted hair, an elbow, a hand with twisted fingers sticking upwards at an angle as if the corpse might be waving.

"No. No-o."

A denial of the scene before me. I turned away, already retching. My stomach was empty and all that came up was strings of bile and stomach acid. Hopper watched me impassively, not stepping forwards to help.

"That is Naimh McCunliffe. She went missing last autumn whilst walking back to her college, Keble, I think. You probably recall it."

Leaning forwards with my hands on my knees I took in a great convulsive breath and nodded. Rain drummed endlessly on the barn roof. He watched me, carefully noting my reactions.

"We've found three bodies buried in barrels out in front of the house, Dr. Garrod, in various states of decay. My team think that there will be more out there, perhaps more in the woods – we're bringing in the ground radar."

He stepped forwards at last, bringing that last photo with him, holding it low so that it was constantly in my eye line, bending slightly so that he could still see my expression.

"When he killed himself, Dr. Jardine did us all a favour. He was a mass murderer. Some of my colleagues think that he had an accomplice, someone to 'help him on his project'. Did he?"

I could barely concentrate on his words. The image in my face – the dead girl robbed of life, robbed of dignity – almost eclipsed them; I shook my head.

The extremity of my reaction must have satisfied Hopper, because he was already taking a step back, ready to place the photograph back on the trestle table, his expression softening, when another voice sounded from the barn door.

"Enough, Hopper."

A tall policewoman made to seem taller by yet another umbrella.

"You've done enough. Not another word."

One more glance at me and Hopper placed the photograph at the table's edge and stalked out through the door. The tall policewoman followed and they stood on the planking in the rain, arguing and gesturing.

Exhausted, I went to the table and sat by it, probably feet from where Jardine had ended his life, and looked out through the door. Rain was everywhere, muddying the air, soaking Hopper and the policewoman in seconds. A gust of wind blew across the scene, taking the rain and the tails of the policewoman's coat with it and a breath of it came in to the barn.

It was getting colder.

I shrugged my phone from my pocked and numbly checked the weather for tomorrow. Sunrise at eight-o-six, sunset at four exactly, high of five, low of minus four, showers all day, becoming wintry by afternoon, turning to snow during the night.

I glanced around me. To my left there was a black stain on the concrete floor. I regarded it dully.

And then you will be me...

I was sitting where Jardine had sat and I was facing the same problem he had faced, the same problem poor Noble had faced, and probably countless others before him. Jardine had entangled me in his crimes enough to make sure that I could not easily flee, and so I was at his mercy as the temperature fell.

Where *was* he? The question kept recurring. Was he out there now, in the world somewhere, waiting, perhaps just over the yew hedge I could see in the distance, sitting behind it in the familiar splay-legged posture that I was now copying, cradling his arm, smiling. Was he in the cold rain or the push and bite of the wind? Was he settled, eyes open in his grave in the black soil?

He was in all of these places and more.

From the table to my right a picture quit its hold and see-sawed lazily down to the dirty barn floor. That tangle of limbs: the student, Naimh. I was struck by fear, such fear that it was painful, as the question dawned in my mind: if he was capable of this horror whilst alive, what could he do now that he was dead, now that his hatred and malice were unbounded. How could you fight the dead?

In the cosy pocket of my coat lay the paring knife. I took it out and tried its keen tip on the ball of my thumb where it dimpled the flesh.

And if somehow I survived this winter, then the world would turn and there would be another, and then another. For me, now, Jardine was as unavoidable as the turning of the earth, as implacable as a gentle fall of snow.

I thought of Ruth, sitting at home, clutching a coffee cup, waiting, or perhaps on a plane, fleeing. A faint tug there, but less than I would have expected.

Wrists would be too slow – Hopper was only feet away, it would have to be an artery: femoral, or more probably carotid, easier to locate, harder to stem, a quicker bleed.

The rain drummed on the roof incessantly and my desperate mind tried to make sense of its randomness by fitting it to patterns of sound that it knew. It was laughter, jagged and hysterical and unending. It was sobbing, dismal and afraid. To the forefront of the sound there was another – a steady and measured drip. I located it. There was a leak in the roof of the barn, high in one back corner. In rain or snow water would come in there. I heard each drop form, reach a swollen, pregnant state, and fall.

It occurred to me that there was a final defeat in this sound. Jardine's visitations had taunted me, not with the sound of his death as I had thought, but with the sound of my own.

I felt for the pulse in my neck and found that its rhythm matched that of the drops, then raised my knife.

Printed in Great Britain
by Amazon.co.uk, Ltd.,
Marston Gate.